ILLUMINATING
Angels

ILLUMINATING *Angels*

Their Story Through Time

LOWRY EDWARDS FOSTER

Illuminating Angels

Published by
Illumify Media Global
www.IllumifyMedia.com
"Let's bring your book to life!"

Paperback ISBN: 978-1-964251-48-6

Typeset by Art Innovations (http://artinnovations.in/)
Cover design by Debbie Lewis
Cover Painting by Morgan Coven Herndon (MCH Artwork)

Printed in the United States of America

DEDICATION

To Yahweh, our creative Maker,
who masterminded everything including angels

CONTENTS

Introduction   9

<u>Old Testament</u>

Chapter 1: The Dawning of Creation   26

Chapter 2: The Devastating Fall   30

Chapter 3: The Cleansing Flood   43

Chapter 4: The Dispersing Nations   52

Chapter 5: The Believing Abraham   61

Chapter 6: The Laughing Isaac   68

Chapter 7: The Conniving Jacob   78

Chapter 8: The Commanding Moses   95

Chapter 9: The Delighting David   104

Chapter 10: The Envisioning Daniel   111

<u>New Testament</u>

Chapter 11: The Astounding Birth   128

Chapter 12: The Legitimizing Temptation   140

Chapter 13: The Agonizing Garden   149

Chapter 14: The Enlivening Closures   157

Chapter 15: The Intervening Activities   166

<u>Ministries</u>

Chapter 16: The Worshiping Ministry   178

Chapter 17: The Praising Ministry   183

Chapter 18: The Informing Ministry   190

Chapter 19: The Serving Ministry   203

Chapter 20: The Protecting Ministry   207

Chapter 21: The Enforcing Ministry   216

<u>Addendum</u>

The Nature of and Facts about Angels   226

<u>Angelology</u>

General Angelology from W. Robert Cook's Theology Outline Notes   230

About the Author   247

INTRODUCTION

Upon commencing to write the chapters of this book, as I had organized them according to the vision Yahweh had given me, I began to ask myself some pertinent questions: Will all my audience (or even most) have a basic knowledge of angels? Is it fair on my part to jump right in with discussion between angels without providing a significant backdrop for them? Even among those familiar in some way with the subject, how logical is it to assume everyone has the same cognizance of angels?

Without an affirmative response to any of this pondering, I quickly concluded this introduction to be of immense importance. However, before presenting clarifying details about the true origins, nature, number, rank, and relationships of angels let us address some commonly held misconceptions. Angels do not resemble the small, chubby, cute depictions by artists who have them shooting little love arrows. As much as many people would like to cling to this perception they have, it remains severely misguided. We will see from Scripture a highly different clear picture of their appearance.

Another belief about angels is the idea that when some of our favorite people die, they become angels watching over us. First, their watching over us requires them to endure much unpleasantness which comes far short of the promised bliss of the afterlife. Also, I think this belief arises out of the inability to let go of loved ones and wanting the best possible outcome for them (and us). Many also put angels in the place of gods or demigods and thus are to be worshipped. After all they seemed to be far superior to mankind with their impressive abilities. But we will see how even angels themselves discourage such worship of themselves. An additional unfounded approach considers angels to be humans who have been given their "wings" for the good deeds they have done as in the movie *It's a Wonderful Life*. Therefore, from this viewpoint, humans are given hope to be able to earn their way to heaven which totally goes against all the scriptural teachings.

Having considered at least a few of the common errors about angels, we will now investigate what the best source—the Bible—conveys to help clarify the subject. Concerning angels being created, the psalmist says:

> "Praise Him, all His angels;
>
> Praise Him, all His hosts!
>
> Praise Him, sun and moon;
>
> Praise Him, all stars of light!
>
> Praise Him, heavens of heavens,
>
> And the waters that are above the heavens!
>
> Let them praise the name of Yahweh,
>
> For He commanded and they were created.

He caused them to stand forever and ever;

He gave a statute and it will never pass away." (Psalm 148:2–6)

Clearly angels were the intended objects in the command God gave for them to be created and were part of His decree. It only took a word on His part and, just like the rest of what He made, angels came into existence. Colossians 1:15–16 provides further evidence: "[Jesus] is the image of the invisible God, the firstborn of all creation. For in Him all things were created, both in the heavens and on earth, visible and invisible, whether thrones or dominions or rulers or authorities—all things have been created through Him and for Him." Absolutely "all things" encompasses angels and thrones and dominions and rulers and authority refers to the ranks among them. The fact that they are created beings is profoundly substantiated. As far as the timeframe of their creation, Exodus 20:11 says: "for in six days Yahweh made heaven and earth, the sea and all that is in them," which included angels.

Job 38:4–7 explains that the morning stars or sons of God, angels, were present when the foundations of the earth were being laid, were being measured, its basis sunk, the cornerstone laid. So, by the process of elimination, we conclude that angels were called into existence during the six days of creation, at least by the third day when the earth or dry land was being formed.

Furthermore, the entire angelic host was created simultaneously and immediately, since angels do not reproduce (Matthew 22:30). And

they are always referred to as sons of God but never as sons of angels. And even though they are called by male names, they are sexless, as is Yahweh Himself.

By nature, they are spirit beings, as Hebrews 1:14, referring to angels, calls them "All ministering spirits." So, they are in essence spirits which infers that they are incorporeal (bodiless). As Jesus explains His spiritual body in Luke 24:39: "See My hands and My feet. See that it is I Myself. Touch Me and see. For a spirit does not have flesh and bones, as you see that I have. "Intrinsically, angels do not live in bodies, but they can assume a human form as needed. This ability has been manifested clearly in Genesis 18 where it says Yahweh appeared before Abraham, and then then says, "three men were standing nearby" (Genesis 18:2). Later it says "the men headed toward Sodom" while Abraham still stood before Yahweh (Genesis 18:22). This becomes clear because "The angel of Yahweh" means an appearance of the pre–Incarnate Christ. Later, Genesis 19:1 describes that the two coming into Sodom were in fact angels and continued to be called such through the remainder of the chapter.

The final characteristics of angels we will discuss herein pertain to their sustenance. They never die as indicated in Luke 20: "[men] cannot even die anymore, because they are like angels and are sons of God, being sons of the resurrection." (Luke 20:36). Although they did have a beginning when they were created, they are imbued with everlasting

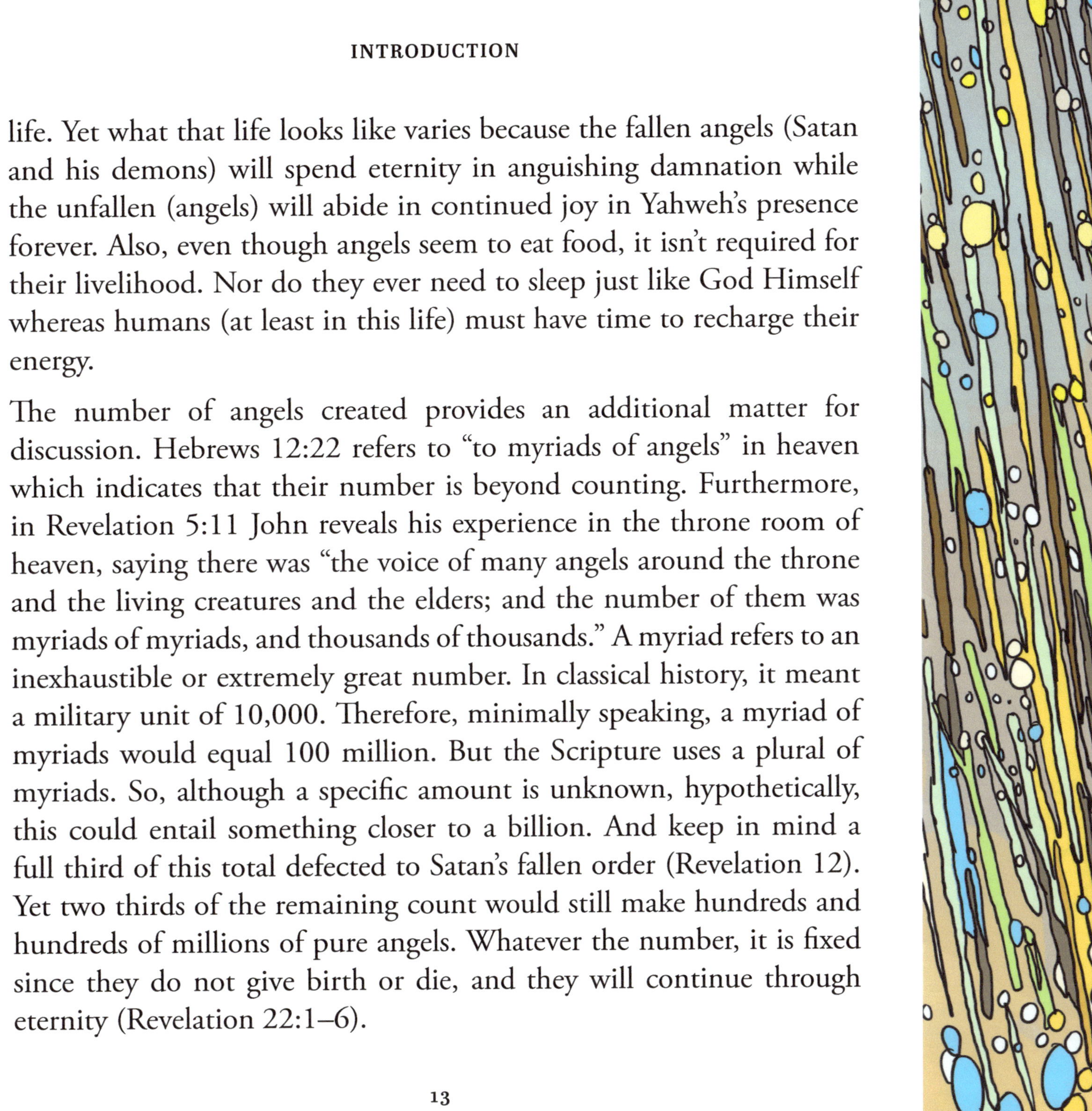

life. Yet what that life looks like varies because the fallen angels (Satan and his demons) will spend eternity in anguishing damnation while the unfallen (angels) will abide in continued joy in Yahweh's presence forever. Also, even though angels seem to eat food, it isn't required for their livelihood. Nor do they ever need to sleep just like God Himself whereas humans (at least in this life) must have time to recharge their energy.

The number of angels created provides an additional matter for discussion. Hebrews 12:22 refers to "to myriads of angels" in heaven which indicates that their number is beyond counting. Furthermore, in Revelation 5:11 John reveals his experience in the throne room of heaven, saying there was "the voice of many angels around the throne and the living creatures and the elders; and the number of them was myriads of myriads, and thousands of thousands." A myriad refers to an inexhaustible or extremely great number. In classical history, it meant a military unit of 10,000. Therefore, minimally speaking, a myriad of myriads would equal 100 million. But the Scripture uses a plural of myriads. So, although a specific amount is unknown, hypothetically, this could entail something closer to a billion. And keep in mind a full third of this total defected to Satan's fallen order (Revelation 12). Yet two thirds of the remaining count would still make hundreds and hundreds of millions of pure angels. Whatever the number, it is fixed since they do not give birth or die, and they will continue through eternity (Revelation 22:1–6).

Now, within their multitude we find structure, but we don't really understand everything we know about it. We believe with certainty (Jude 9) that Michael holds the title of archangel, meaning he rules over all angels. That's also confirmed in Daniel 10:13. Gabriel may also belong to this position as well since he clarifies for Zachariah the validity of his message by stating, "I am Gabriel who stands before God" (Luke 1:19). This privilege may be granted to other angels as well, but it seems to set Gabriel apart with special honor. Various passages specify there are recognized orders including rulers, authorities, powers, dominions, etc. (Ephesians 1:21, 6:12; Colossians 1:16, 2:15). Some are called the prince of a certain country, such as Persia (Daniel 10:13). There still much remains to learn about these titles.

Finally, let us consider how angels relate to men. First, they must not be defined as glorified human beings. The author of Hebrews distinguishes between angels and mankind (Hebrews 12:22–23). In two other locations in the Word we are told men are like angels, but not being the equivalent to angels (Matthew 22:30 and Luke 20:36). Furthermore, their sphere places them higher than man (Psalm 8:4–5; Hebrews 2:5–8) due to their essence being pure spirit and thus of a different created order. Other examples which further differentiate them from humankind include how they rejoice over the salvation of men (Luke 15:10) and that they will be judged by the saints (1 Corinthians 6:3).

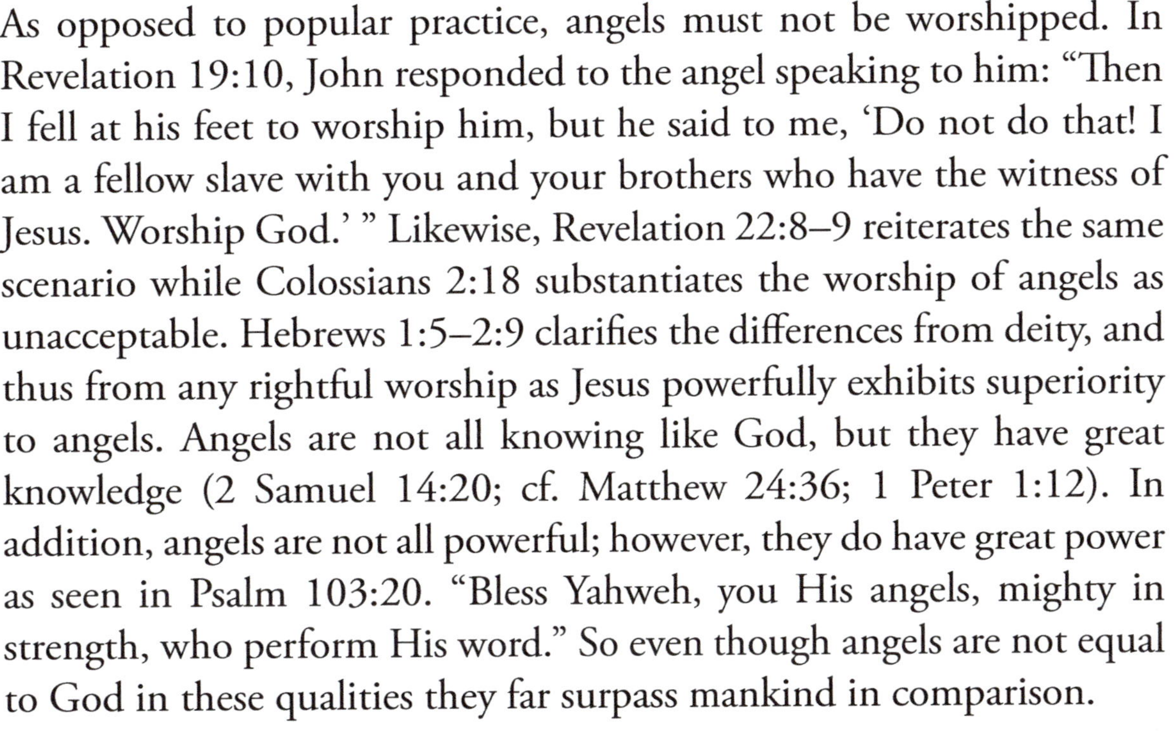

As opposed to popular practice, angels must not be worshipped. In Revelation 19:10, John responded to the angel speaking to him: "Then I fell at his feet to worship him, but he said to me, 'Do not do that! I am a fellow slave with you and your brothers who have the witness of Jesus. Worship God.' " Likewise, Revelation 22:8–9 reiterates the same scenario while Colossians 2:18 substantiates the worship of angels as unacceptable. Hebrews 1:5–2:9 clarifies the differences from deity, and thus from any rightful worship as Jesus powerfully exhibits superiority to angels. Angels are not all knowing like God, but they have great knowledge (2 Samuel 14:20; cf. Matthew 24:36; 1 Peter 1:12). In addition, angels are not all powerful; however, they do have great power as seen in Psalm 103:20. "Bless Yahweh, you His angels, mighty in strength, who perform His word." So even though angels are not equal to God in these qualities they far surpass mankind in comparison.

Most of you are familiar with historical fiction. Paradoxically, this book is biblical fiction. What I mean by that is that its foundation is on the Scriptures, but then I take literary license to expound interactions between angels that are not actually in the Scriptures. Not that what the angels say is anti-biblical and although it isn't directly from the Bible, it is in keeping with what we know about Yahweh and His messengers. For example, what I have the angels say sometimes isn't in the Word directly, and yet it is in keeping with their character and how Yahweh created them.

I'm a big fan of J. R. R. Tolkien and C. S. Lewis and have researched their writing extensively. When Yahweh kept reminding me that they both wrote fiction, I responded by acknowledging this. At the same time, I expressed that if I wrote fiction, I wouldn't have any idea what it would be about. Then while driving home from visiting my daughters, He suggested angels. This resounded with me and felt this was something I could accomplish with His help. Shortly thereafter, I began to formulate a plan for implementing this process. After reading each passage regarding angels, I began to place each one in a category and out of that came an outline for the book. I pleaded with Yahweh to give me a creative approach and the thought came to have the two named angels discussing the events of history and calling upon other angels who were on location. This then became the basis for my approach in the book throughout.

Billy Graham, the renowned preacher, acknowledges the validity of the subject in his 2001 book *Angels* when he wrote: "Angels have a much more important place in the Bible than the devil and his demons. Therefore, I undertook a biblical study of the subject of angels. Not only has it been one of the most fascinating studies of my life, but I believe the subject is more relevant today than perhaps at any time in history."

Therefore, let us begin with an examination of the types of angels' ministries. That is, those categories in which they function or do not.

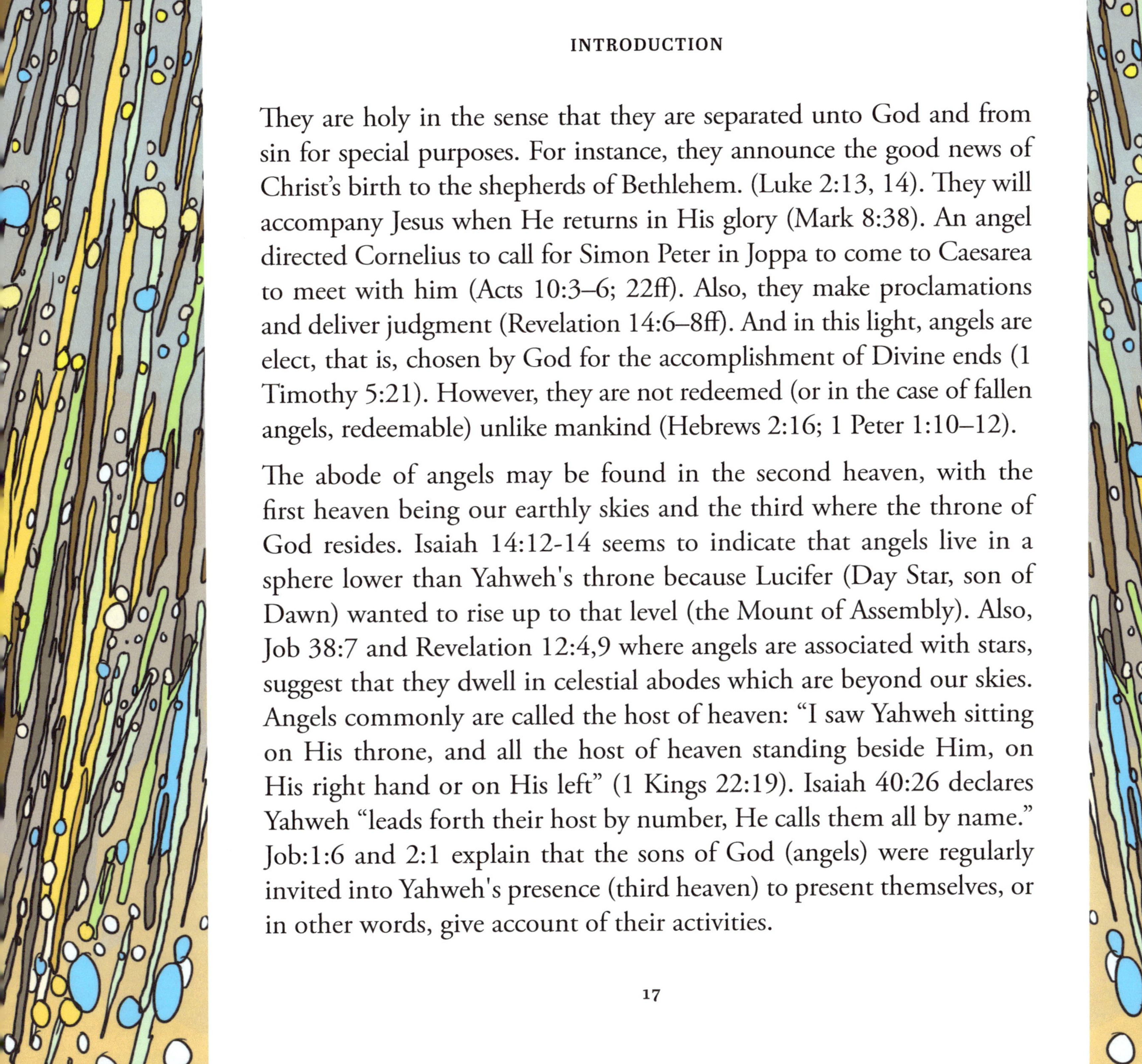

They are holy in the sense that they are separated unto God and from sin for special purposes. For instance, they announce the good news of Christ's birth to the shepherds of Bethlehem. (Luke 2:13, 14). They will accompany Jesus when He returns in His glory (Mark 8:38). An angel directed Cornelius to call for Simon Peter in Joppa to come to Caesarea to meet with him (Acts 10:3–6; 22ff). Also, they make proclamations and deliver judgment (Revelation 14:6–8ff). And in this light, angels are elect, that is, chosen by God for the accomplishment of Divine ends (1 Timothy 5:21). However, they are not redeemed (or in the case of fallen angels, redeemable) unlike mankind (Hebrews 2:16; 1 Peter 1:10–12).

The abode of angels may be found in the second heaven, with the first heaven being our earthly skies and the third where the throne of God resides. Isaiah 14:12-14 seems to indicate that angels live in a sphere lower than Yahweh's throne because Lucifer (Day Star, son of Dawn) wanted to rise up to that level (the Mount of Assembly). Also, Job 38:7 and Revelation 12:4,9 where angels are associated with stars, suggest that they dwell in celestial abodes which are beyond our skies. Angels commonly are called the host of heaven: "I saw Yahweh sitting on His throne, and all the host of heaven standing beside Him, on His right hand or on His left" (1 Kings 22:19). Isaiah 40:26 declares Yahweh "leads forth their host by number, He calls them all by name." Job:1:6 and 2:1 explain that the sons of God (angels) were regularly invited into Yahweh's presence (third heaven) to present themselves, or in other words, give account of their activities.

Regarding the multiple ways angels minister, it all begins with their name. Both in Hebrew and in Greek, the word *angel* means "one who brings a message," "a messenger." This means their service may be relegated into categories which may overlap in many cases.

The first we will acknowledge depicts angels unequivocally worshipping Yahweh. Psalm 99:1 amplifies this activity when it states: "Yahweh reigns, let the peoples tremble; He sits enthroned above the cherubim." In other words, these angels continually exalt him. We are commanded to join in with their efforts: "Exalt Yahweh our God. Worship at His footstool! Holy is He!" (Psalm 99:5).

Isaiah 6:1–3 creates a graphic throne room scene: "I saw the Lord sitting on a throne, high and lifted up, with the train of His robe filling the temple. Seraphim stood above Him, each having six wings: with two he covered his face, and with two he covered his feet, and with two he flew. And one called out to another and said, 'Holy, Holy, Holy, is Yahweh of hosts; The whole earth is full of His glory.' " One final example of this ministry is found in Revelation 5:11-14: "Then I looked, and I heard the voice of many angels around the throne and the living creatures and the elders; and the number of them was myriads of myriads, and thousands of thousands, saying with a loud voice, 'Worthy is the Lamb that was slain to receive power and riches and wisdom and strength and honor and glory and blessing.' . . . And the four living creatures kept saying, 'Amen.' And the elders fell down and worshiped." So, the core

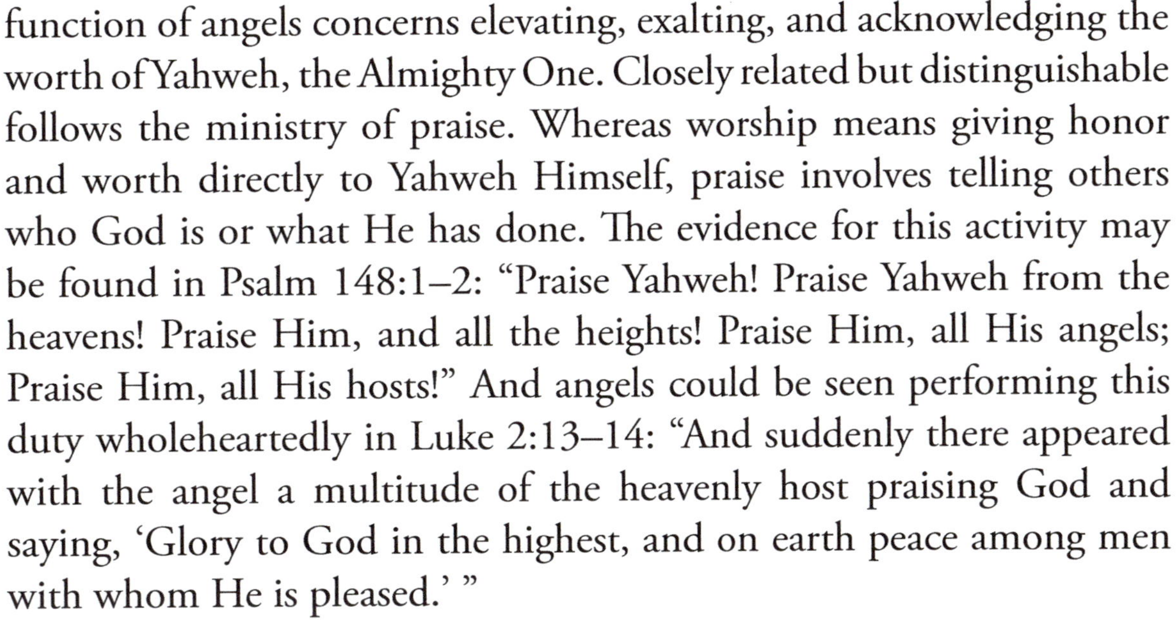

function of angels concerns elevating, exalting, and acknowledging the worth of Yahweh, the Almighty One. Closely related but distinguishable follows the ministry of praise. Whereas worship means giving honor and worth directly to Yahweh Himself, praise involves telling others who God is or what He has done. The evidence for this activity may be found in Psalm 148:1–2: "Praise Yahweh! Praise Yahweh from the heavens! Praise Him, and all the heights! Praise Him, all His angels; Praise Him, all His hosts!" And angels could be seen performing this duty wholeheartedly in Luke 2:13–14: "And suddenly there appeared with the angel a multitude of the heavenly host praising God and saying, 'Glory to God in the highest, and on earth peace among men with whom He is pleased.' "

Thus, the angels demonstrated how to proclaim the wonders of Yahweh to everyone within the range of their voices.

Next, let's examine the general category of serving and consider how and to whom these beings serve. First, angels minister to the elect, and even before their salvation as seen in Hebrews 1:14: "Are they not all ministering spirits, sent to render service for the sake of those who will inherit salvation?" Second, angels have a ministry to the churches as seen in Revelation 1:20; 2:1, 8, 12, 18; 3:1 7, 14. Apparently there is an angel assigned to each particular church, and they look out for those in that congregation, just like how it was in all the churches of Asia Minor, whom John addressed in the first chapters of Revelation.

The third category of serving relates to Israel. Thus, in Daniel 12:1 we are told "Michael, the great prince who stands guard over the sons of [Daniel's] people," indicating his special concern for Israel. Also, angels were present at the giving of the law in Acts 7:53. And in the future, they will gather elect Israel at the time of Christ's second coming, seen in Matthew 24:31.

The fourth dimension of angel's serving references their care for children. Matthew 18:10 explains "See that you do not despise one of these little ones, for I say to you that their angels in heaven continually see the face of My Father who is in heaven." We may then conclude that children as a group at least have angels guarding over them.

Fifthly, some angels give special attention to their nations. This clearly is developed In Daniel 10, 11, and 12 when Daniel, who had been interceding regarding the visions he was receiving, is visited by Gabriel, who comes to explain the spiritual battle going on behind the scenes. Gabriel had been battling the prince (demon) of the kingdom of Persia and was finally supported by Michael whose primary concern was Israel. This spiritual warfare takes place obviously out of sight and continually Yahweh contends with the forces of evil. Therefore, in another sense, the guardian angel concept may be affirmed. Also verified in Psalm 91:11–12 where we are told: "For He will command His angels concerning you, to guard you in all your ways. On their hands they will bear you up, lest you strike your foot against a stone."

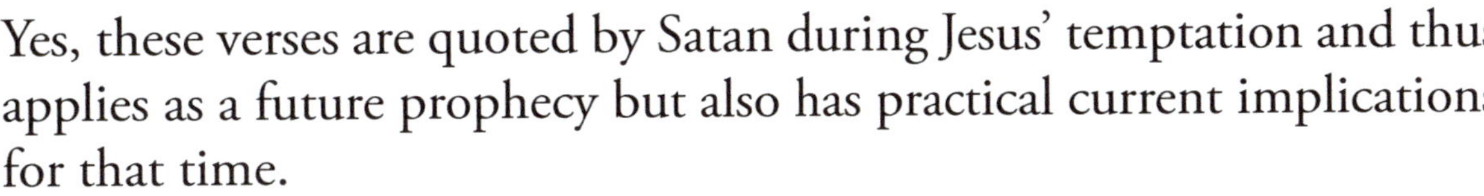

Yes, these verses are quoted by Satan during Jesus' temptation and thus applies as a future prophecy but also has practical current implications for that time.

A vitally important ministry for angels concerns that which they had or will have in their extensive care for Jesus. At His birth (Luke 2:13), following the temptation (Matthew 4:11), in the garden (Luke 22:43), at the ascension (Acts 1:10), at the rapture (1 Thessalonians 4:16), at the second coming (Matthew 25:31; 2 Thessalonians 1:7).

Another not-to-be-forgotten responsibility of angels is how they protect and deliver. When two angels came to check on the wickedness of Sodom and were attacked, they "reached out their hands and brought Lot into the house with them and shut the door. And they struck the men who were at the doorway of the house with blindness, from small to great, so that they wearied themselves trying to find the doorway" (Genesis 19:10–11). And so it was that the angels rescued Lot from the evil intent of his town's people.

In the story of the three Hebrew princes, they were covered by an angel in the fiery furnace. And another angel shut the mouth of the lions to rescue Daniel (Daniel 3:28; 6:22). The apostles in the New Testament were freed from prison by an angel (Acts 5:19; 12:7–11) on multiple occasions.

When Elijah fled from Jezebel in terror, after he had run hundreds of miles and was in danger of collapsing, an angel appeared with sustenance

twice to nourish him (1 Kings 19:5–8). Also, when Elisha, Elijah's protege, was surrounded by a huge Syrian army, He asked Yahweh to open his servant's eyes to see. "For those who are with us are more than those who are with them." And when his eyes were open "He saw; and behold, the mountain was full of horses and chariots of fire all around Elisha" (2 Kings 6:16–17). A similar situation occurred when Sennacherib, king of Assyria, besieged Jerusalem and Yahweh sent an angel to destroy 185,000 (2 Kings 19:3–5).

Additionally, other times angels were sent to inform, direct, and encourage, such as when an angel (or two) rolled back the stone at the tomb and sat on it:

> "And his appearance was like lightning, and his clothing as white as snow. And the guards quaked from fear of him and became like dead men. And the angel answered and said to the women, "Do not be afraid; for I know that you are looking for Jesus who has been crucified. He is not here, for He has risen, just as He said. Come, see the place where He was lying. And go quickly and tell His disciples that He has risen from the dead; and behold, He is going ahead of you into Galilee, there you will see Him; behold, I have told you."
> (Matthew 28:3–7)

At another time when God was arranging help for the Ethiopian Eunuch in Acts, He sent an angel to guide him to a place where he would meet Phillip, one of the deacons chosen to serve the body but

who also was quite an evangelist. So, Phillip completed the Ethiopians education about the Scriptures which led him to being baptized (Acts 8:25–39).

A curious quality the angels often demonstrated involved observation. They watched diligently to see how women project their submission to man's authority by her covering on her head (1 Corinthians 11:10). They also learn about the "manifold wisdom of God" through the church (Ephesians 3:10). And they yearn to understand salvation, which they have never experienced (1 Peter 1:12).

A final service for Yahweh shows they function as instruments of His judgment which will receive particular attention at the conclusion of this book. Peoples are destroyed (Genesis 19:12–13), a pestilence comes against Israel for David's sin of numbering Israel (2 Samuel 24:16), enemies are devastated (2 Kings 19:35), executing justice on the guilty of Israel (Ezekiel 9:1; Matthew 13:36–42, 49–50). As you can surmise, the activities of angels are diverse and detailed.

John Calvin summarized it well in volume 1 of his *Institutes of Christian Religion* when he said, "Angels are the dispensers and administrators of the divine beneficence toward us. They regard our safety, undertake our defense, direct our ways, and exercise a constant solicitude that no evil befall us."

OLD TESTAMENT

CHAPTER 1

THE DAWNING OF CREATION

"Then Yahweh answered Job out of the whirlwind and said . . .

'Where were you when I laid the foundation of the earth?

Tell me, if you know understanding.

Who set its measurements? Since you know.

Or who stretched the line upon it?

On what were its bases sunk?

Or who laid its cornerstone,

when the morning stars sang together

and all the sons of God shouted for joy?' " (Job. 38:1–7)

א

Aleph

MICHAEL: Let us exalt the Most High forever, Gabriel. Let us recall how our first memories following our creation were filled with awe and wonder as Yahweh spoke into existence more of His vision.

GABRIEL: Yes, Michael, the Maker's flawless design became reality in those initial moments. I felt so favored to be a witness to Yah's unmatched genius as He laid out His plans for making the earth out of nothing.

MICHAEL: Our Master always deserves all praise and glory from all His creatures for who He is as well as all that He has done. I particularly revere Him for how He used water from the face of the deep to create the dry land.

GABRIEL: I am amazed at the way the Spirit of God hovered over the waters in the beginning. And then Yahweh spoke light into place, emanating from His own person. How spectacular was it for Him to separate the light from the darkness, calling the light day and the darkness night.

MICHAEL: What is so fascinating to me is the pronouncing that evening then morning completed the first day. And, as only God could, He separated the waters into heavens above from those below by means of a canopy.

GABRIEL: Yes, absolutely, the canopy provided a wonderful protection for this new world, and a second day was manifested. But that wasn't all, the Designer collected all the waters below into seas and the dry land—earth—appeared.

MICHAEL: And after producing vegetation from the ground, He called it another day and declared it good. I can surely see why. Following this first light, water, earth sequence, the cycle repeated for the next three days.

GABRIEL: Exactly, Michael. Yahweh then proceeded to speak lights into the heavens, with the sun to rule by day, and the moon and the stars to watch over the night. On the fifth day, He created inhabitants for the skies and waters.

MICHAEL: And to bring completion, Yahweh populated the earth with all types of animals. What an amazing assortment of styles and colors. His attention to detail fully demonstrates the magnitude of His complexity!

GABRIEL: Then He topped off this creation week with His ultimate work—the man and his wife whom He placed in charge over all of the creation.

MICHAEL: Yahweh's final comment on His creation labeled everything that was made "Very good." Nothing could be a higher commendation than from the Almighty Himself!

GABRIEL: Then Lucifer changed all that.

"God blessed them, and God said to them, 'Be fruitful and multiply, and fill the earth, and subdue it; and have dominion over the fish of the sea and over the birds of the sky and over every living thing that creeps on the earth.' Then God said, 'Behold, I have given to you every plant yielding seed that is on the surface of all the earth, and every tree which has the fruit of the tree yielding seed; it shall be food for you; and to every beast of the earth and to every bird of the sky and to every thing that creeps on the earth which has life, I have given every green plant for food'; and it was so. And God saw all that He had made, and behold, it was very good. And there was evening and there was morning, the sixth day." (Genesis 1:28-31)

CHAPTER 2

THE DEVASTATING FALL

"Now the serpent was more crafty than any beast of the field which Yahweh God had made. And he said to the woman, 'Indeed, has God said, "You shall not eat from any tree of the garden"?' And the woman said to the serpent, 'From the fruit of the trees of the garden we may eat; but from the fruit of the tree which is in the midst of the garden, God said, "You shall not eat from it, and you shall not touch it, lest you die." ' And the serpent said to the woman, 'You surely will not die! For God knows that in the day you eat from it your eyes will be opened, and you will be like God, knowing good and evil.' Then the woman saw that the tree was good for food, and that it was a delight to the eyes, and that the tree was desirable to make one wise, so she took from its fruit and ate; and she gave also to her husband with her, and he ate." (Genesis 3:1-6)

ב

Beth

MICHAEL: Sadly, everything changed. We were designated as archangels over all the other angels. But Lucifer—the Morning Star—was even higher than us as he was to lead worship of our King; however, he had even greater aspirations.

GABRIEL: Unfortunately, he immediately had designs on being worshipped himself and wanted to be like the Most High.

MICHAEL: A clear description in Ezekiel's prophecy (28:12) declared Lucifer as "the seal of perfection, full of wisdom and perfect in beauty" and details his placement as "anointed cherub who covers."

GABRIEL: Of course, Ezekiel also noted his being blameless in all his ways "from the day [he] was created."

MICHAEL: And Isaiah's vision (14:12) names him as "star of the morning, son of the dawn," in other words, as light-bringer for all of Yahweh's creation.

GABRIEL: So being the most beautiful of all of us "stars," this "son of God" became enamored with himself and lusted for even more power than he had already been given.

MICHAEL: He declared in his heart, as Isaiah conveys (14 the five I wills: "I will ascend to heaven; I will raise my throne above the stars

of God, And I will sit on the mount of assembly in the recesses of the north. I will ascend above the heights of the clouds; I will make myself like the Most High."

GABRIEL: Thus, unrighteousness was found in him. Ezekiel says: "In the abundance of your trade you were filled with violence in your midst, and you sinned" (28:18).

MICHAEL: Yes, and he even managed to convince a third of us—hundreds of thousands of angels—to join him in rebellion against the Holy One!

GABRIEL: True, but Yahweh could not put up with such evil and immediately cast the deceiver, Satan, or the devil, as he is now called, along with his impure cohorts, out of His presence and down to earth.

MICHAEL: What a disgrace! We could scarcely fathom the depths of this atrocity against the Most Perfect!

GABRIEL: And yet those of us who remain pure knew whom we serve, and it was our duty to fight against the evil ones.

MICHAEL: Yes, we led the righteous host of angels against the dragon—the ancient serpent—and his unholy companions.

GABRIEL: And, of course, we know who won this war in heaven. The consequence for those rebels meant there was no longer a place for them in heaven, and so they were cast down to the earth.

MICHAEL: Now the devil and his demons began to carry out his plan on earth to thwart Yahweh's promises. The first evidence: when the serpent approached Eve in the Garden of Eden.

GABRIEL: He sought to undermine her trust in Yahweh by suggesting half-truths and questioning God's intentions. Did Yahweh really mean you would die by simply eating of the forbidden fruit?

MICHAEL: Why was Yahweh withholding something obviously desirable? Didn't He have their good at heart? Thus, this illustrates his new name as a deceiver in opposition to God's designs.

GABRIEL: Right and he also demonstrates his apt title—Satan—because now he becomes the accuser of the brethren.

MICHAEL: In Job's story, Satan represents himself along with all the sons of God before Yahweh. When asked by Yahweh where he has come from, he answers, "from roaming about on the earth and walking around on it" (1:7).

GABRIEL: Then Yahweh asked Satan, "Have you set your heart upon My servant Job? For there is no one like him on the earth, a blameless and upright man, fearing God and turning away from evil?"

Michael. Satan answers. "Does Job fear God without cause? Have you not made a hedge around him and his house and all that he has, on every side?"

GABRIEL: Satan went on to say, "You have blessed the work of his hands, and his possessions have increased in the land. But send forth Your hand and touch all that he has; he will surely curse You to your face."

MICHAEL: Yahweh then replied, "Behold, all that he has is in your hand. Only against him do not send forth your hand." And, with this freedom, Satan then went out from the presence of Yahweh.

GABRIEL: When these efforts by Satan did not accomplish his desired end, he came back on another day to present himself before Yahweh with the same interaction.

MICHAEL: Yes, I remember how Yahweh challenged Satan again saying, "Have you set your heart upon My servant Job? For there is no one like him on the earth, a blameless and upright man, fearing God and

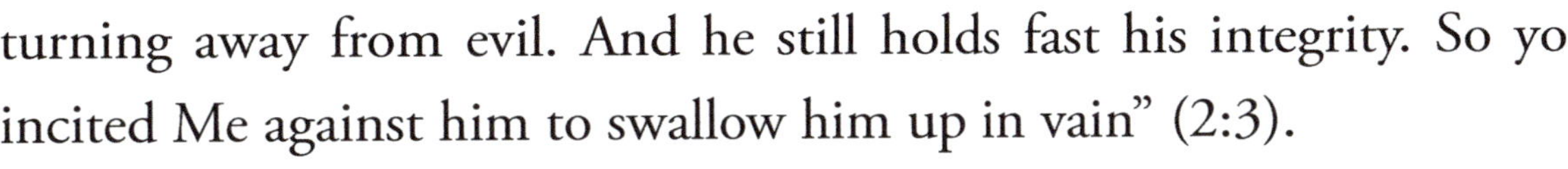

turning away from evil. And he still holds fast his integrity. So you incited Me against him to swallow him up in vain" (2:3).

GABRIEL: Satan answered Yahweh and said, "Skin for skin! Yes, all that a man has, he will give for his life. However, send forth Your hand now and touch his bone and his flesh; he will curse You to Your face" (2:4).

MICHAEL: And Yahweh said to Satan, "Behold, he is in your hand, only spare his life." So, Satan went out from the presence of Yahweh and struck Job.

GABRIEL: Therefore, the apostle Peter in the New Testament appropriately exhorts, "Be of sober *spirit*, be watchful. Your adversary, the devil, prowls around like a roaring lion, seeking someone to devour" (1 Peter 5:8).

MICHAEL: And the apostle Paul warns "not to give the devil an opportunity" (Ephesians 4:27). In addition, the apostle James challenges believers to "resist the devil and he will flee from you" (James 4:7).

GABRIEL: Paul also encourages that we, "Put on the whole armor of God, so that you may be able to stand firm against the schemes of the devil" (Ephesians 6:11). And, then we're told in verse 12: "For our struggle is not against flesh and blood, but against the rulers, against

the authorities, against the world forces of this darkness, against the spiritual forces of wickedness in the heavenly places."

MICHAEL: Paul also reiterates that "the weapons of our warfare are not of the flesh but divinely powerful for the tearing down of strongholds" (2 Corinthians 10:4).

GABRIEL: Yes, Paul also acknowledges this world is following "the ruler of the power of the air, the spirit that is now at work in the sons of disobedience" (Ephesians 2:2).

MICHAEL: And to think it all began in the Garden of Eden with Adam and Eve, when the serpent initiated his plan to corrupt God's creation.

GABRIEL: No surprise, Satan shrewdly chose the serpent who was the craftiest of the beasts of the field. He possessed this creature for his own evil purpose and began to speak through it.

MICHAEL: He started by questioning what God really said to Adam and Eve: "Indeed, has God said, 'You shall not eat from any tree of the garden'?" (Genesis 3:1).

GABRIEL: Well, of course, God didn't warn them to not eat from all of the trees in the garden. And Eve answered: "From the fruit of the trees

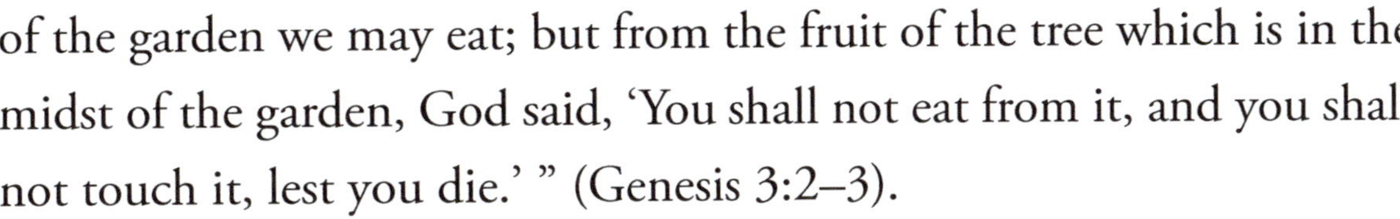

of the garden we may eat; but from the fruit of the tree which is in the midst of the garden, God said, 'You shall not eat from it, and you shall not touch it, lest you die.' " (Genesis 3:2–3).

MICHAEL: Here she inserted her own lie, because God had not told them not to touch it, only not eat it. And now Satan builds on that by saying, "You surely will not die! For God knows when you eat of it your eyes will be open, and you will be like God, knowing good and evil" (3:4–5).

GABRIEL: At that point, she "saw that the tree was good for food, and that it was a delight to the eyes, and that the tree was desirable to make one wise, so she took from its fruit and ate; and she gave also to her husband with her, and he ate " (3:6).

MICHAEL: Consequently, the eyes of both were open, and they knew that they were naked. And they sewed fig leaves together and made themselves loin cloths.

GABRIEL: So, Eve was deceived by Satan's tricky arguments and Adam did not fulfill his leadership role to protect her; he just complied with her choices.

MICHAEL: The implications became clear when they encountered Yahweh seeking them in the garden. They were obviously guilty and ashamed, so they attempted to hide themselves from His presence—a ridiculous move on their part.

GABRIEL: Yahweh then called out to the man, "Where are you?" Which really meant "Why are you where you are?" (3:9). For God surely knew where they were located.

MICHAEL: Adam feebly attempted to answer God by saying, "I heard the sound of You in the garden and I was afraid, because I was naked; so I hid" (3:10). Obviously, nakedness indicated vulnerability, which they now were aware of.

GABRIEL: Yahweh replied with two questions: "Who told you that you were naked? Have you eaten of the tree of which I commanded you not to eat?" (3:11).

MICHAEL: At that point Adam tried to put the blame on Eve and God: "The woman whom You gave to be with me, she gave me the fruit of the tree, and I ate" (3:12).

GABRIEL: Then Yahweh addressed the woman: "What is it that you have done?" And she put the blame elsewhere, too: "The serpent deceived me, and I ate" (3:13).

MICHAEL: Yahweh responded with His judgment for each, beginning with the serpent, then the woman, and finally with Adam.

GABRIEL: The serpent (and thus Satan too) was cursed to now crawl on his belly all his life, and eat dust—that is, be subject to all others. Ultimately, he would be crushed beneath the foot of woman's offspring—Jesus. And Jesus was to be bruised in the heel by Satan.

MICHAEL: We saw that brought to fruition with Jesus going to the cross and paying a mighty price. Nevertheless, He came out victorious over sin and death!

GABRIEL: Yahweh's judgment for the woman included increased pain in childbirth from what it was intended to be initially. Also, she would desire to rule over her husband and yet he would still have dominion over her as Eve was deceived by Satan and not Adam.

MICHAEL: Then it became Adam's turn to be judged, and since he listened to his wife's voice and not God's command not to eat the fruit,

the ground was cursed for him. This meant he would have to labor with much more difficulty to get the food he needed to live.

GABRIEL: Yes, and now Yahweh vowed that man would now return to the dust from which he was made when he died. Even with how Adam and Eve profoundly failed Yahweh, He still made provision for them— clothes of animal skin to cover them.

MICHAEL: This had huge implications for them because it was another sign of how God would provide for their salvation through blood shed on their behalf.

GABRIEL: Yahweh now acknowledged that the man and the woman had become like God in knowing the difference between good and evil.

MICHAEL: Therefore, to keep them from eternally damning themselves by eating also of the tree of life, they were sent out from the garden. No longer would they be tempted by this option, since the way to the tree of life would now be guarded by our cherubim and the flaming sword.

GABRIEL: So that's the history of our creation and the subsequent fall of Lucifer and his angels. All of this came to bear on the newly formed Adam and Eve.

MICHAEL: That was a lot to cover, but well worth the reminder. Obviously not all of the discussion was pleasant, and yet it is important for perspective on the backdrop of sin.

GABRIEL: This also provides a contrast with the conclusion yet to come and how our Master, Yahweh, overcomes all this evil. We look forward to sharing these wonderful truths as well.

"For the wrath of God is revealed from heaven against all ungodliness and unrighteousness of men who suppress the truth in unrighteousness, because that which is known about God is evident within them; for God made it evident to them. For since the creation of the world His invisible attributes, both His eternal power and divine nature, have been clearly seen, being understood through what has been made, so that they are without excuse. For even though they knew God, they did not glorify Him as God or give thanks, but they became futile in their thoughts, and their foolish heart was darkened. Professing to be wise, they became fools, and exchanged the glory of the incorruptible God for an image in the likeness of corruptible man and of birds and four-footed animals and crawling creatures.

"Therefore God gave them over in the lusts of their hearts to impurity, so that their bodies would be dishonored among them. For they exchanged the truth of God for a lie, and worshiped and served the creature rather than the Creator, who is blessed forever. Amen." (Romans 1:18–25)

CHAPTER 3

THE CLEANSING FLOOD

"When men began to multiply on the face of the land, and daughters were born to them, that the sons of God saw that the daughters of men were good in appearance; and they took wives for themselves, whomever they chose. Then Yahweh said, 'My Spirit shall not strive with man forever because he indeed is flesh; nevertheless his days shall be 120 years.' The Nephilim were on the earth in those days, and also afterward, when the sons of God came in to the daughters of men, and they bore children to them. Those were the mighty men who were of old, men of renown.

"Then Yahweh saw that the evil of man was great on the earth, and that every intent of the thoughts of his heart was only evil continually. And Yahweh regretted that He had made man on the earth, and He was grieved in His heart. And Yahweh said, 'I will blot out man whom I have created from the face of the land, from man to animals to creeping things and to birds of the sky; for I regret that I have made them.' But Noah found favor in the eyes of Yahweh. . . .

"Now the earth was corrupt before God, and the earth was filled with violence. And God saw the earth, and behold, it was corrupt; for all flesh had corrupted their way upon the earth.

"Then God said to Noah, 'The end of all flesh has come before Me; for the earth is filled with violence because of them; and behold, I am about to destroy them with the earth.'" (Genesis 6:1–8,11–13)

ג

Gimel

MICHAEL: It took only nine generations for the seed of corruption sown by Satan through Adam and Eve to dominate all of creation.

GABRIEL: Yahweh, having seen the evil spreading for many years, took stock of how all this had come to a culmination.

MICHAEL: Yes, Gabriel, Yahweh had demonstrated long-suffering toward His creation, and now that was going to come to an end.

GABRIEL: Michael, as you know, the activity that finally resulted in punitive judgment by our Master began with some of His angels who had already fallen, pushing the limit further.

MICHAEL: A group of rebel angels found the daughters of men to be desirable, and their lust toward them resulted in their taking them for their own as they chose.

GABRIEL: Some may wonder how this could be possible since we angels are spirits in essence and therefore do not have permanent physical bodies.

MICHAEL: Absolutely, and the answer may be derived from what took place in the garden and reaffirmed at many other junctures throughout time.

GABRIEL: Satan, being spirit, has no tangible flesh, and so we see that he chose to occupy an animal—the serpent. This allowed him to manifest himself in a corporal display.

MICHAEL: The serpent even used human speech, which does not comply with the normal animal physics but became possible when Satan's spirit possessed the creature.

GABRIEL: Thus, when the sons of God, who are always depicted as angels, wanted these human women, they took over the bodies of human men, and consequently they could perform their bodily functions.

MICHAEL: Yahweh's initial response entailed reducing the length of man's life from what had been around 1,000 years to just 120. This was to reduce the effect of this evil at least to a shorter timeframe.

GABRIEL: And we see the extended judgment on these angels (demons) described by several New Testament apostles.

MICHAEL: Jude states clearly that " the angels who did not keep their own domain, but abandoned their proper abode, He has kept in eternal bonds under darkness for the judgment of the great day" (Jude 1:6).

GABRIEL: Furthermore, the apostle Peter referred to the same sequence of events when he wrote that "if God did not spare angels who sinned, but cast them into the pit and delivered them to chains of darkness, being kept for judgment" (2 Peter 2:4), what is going to happen to the ungodly?

MICHAEL: He goes on to say in that the Lord knows how to "rescue the godly from trial, and to keep the unrighteous under punishment for the day of judgment, and especially those who go after the flesh in its corrupt lust and despise authority" (2:9–10).

GABRIEL: So, despite the future consequences these angels produce a huge ill-effect on the world at this time. The Nephilim, giants, were the offspring of demons having sexual relations with the daughters of men.

MICHAEL: These hybrid demon-human progeny wreaked havoc on Yahweh's creation and plan, and their superhuman effort made them legend as "mighty men of old, the men of renown." Most assuredly they were well-known for the wrong reasons or what we might call infamous.

GABRIEL: Obviously these "men" had capabilities well beyond the normal skills of plain humans, and they were recognized as such. You might even say they were worshipped as gods.

MICHAEL: Satan's attempts to ruin Yahweh's plan certainly seemed to be working, and God acknowledged it as such.

GABRIEL: Yahweh observed that man's wickedness had grown so prevalent that not only their actions, but intents of the thoughts of their hearts were only evil continually (Genesis 6:5).

MICHAEL: So, Yahweh drew a conclusion that because He was so full of sorrow—and grieved that He had even created man and animals, He would have no better option than to start over.

GABRIEL: Yes, He had determined it was best to blot out all His creation. And the animals were included in this corruption because, like the serpent, they too had been possessed by demons.

MICHAEL: In fact, that explains how we ended up with dinosaurs. Not only were men now polluted by devils inhabiting them but so were the animals.

GABRIEL: Therefore, they also became giants and went from eating only plants as designed, to devouring flesh instead. Thus only violence filled the earth.

MICHAEL: Let us be reminded that when Yahweh had finished creating, He gave an exhortation to Adam and Eve to be fruitful and multiply and fill the earth and subdue it (Genesis 1:28).

GABRIEL: Yes, they were commanded to have dominion over everything on earth. Then they were given specific instructions about their food.

MICHAEL: They were told that every plant yielding seed had fruit which was given to them for their sustenance (1:29).

GABRIEL: And every beast and bird, including all who had the breath of life, He also gave them every green plant for food.

MICHAEL: Therefore, every creature was originally meant to only eat vegetation. But by the time of the flood this had all changed and flesh was eating flesh and thus the violence was at hand.

GABRIEL: Satan had effectively spoiled the earth; it had become polluted except for Noah, whom Yahweh had given the gift of righteousness through His favor.

MICHAEL: Clearly Noah responded to this grace given by Yahweh by consequently walking blamelessly with Him. The rest of the earth was a whole different picture. Let us hear directly from those who were on location: Uriel and Raphael.

URIEL: We were up close and personal as we all watched as this catastrophe develop before our eyes. Our King witnessed that the

earth was completely corrupt to the extent that it was only filled with violence.

Raphael: Then the Master explained to Noah His plan in response to the corruption. He was to make an end of all flesh.

Gabriel: Furthermore, He felt the need to carry out this judgment because the earth was full of violence through all His creatures and not just men.

Michael: All his creatures were involved in complete depravity due to the influence and possession by Satan and his demons. Therefore, they would reap the justice due them to cleanse the earth.

"For if God did not spare angels who sinned, but cast them into the pit and delivered them to chains of darkness, being kept for judgment; and did not spare the ancient world, but preserved Noah, a preacher of righteousness, with seven others, when He brought a flood upon the world of the ungodly." (2 Peter 2:4–5)

CHAPTER 4

THE DISPERSING NATIONS

"Now the whole earth had the same language, and the same words. And it happened as they journeyed east, that they found a plain in the land of Shinar and settled there. Then they said to one another, 'Come, let us make bricks, and burn them thoroughly.' And they had brick for stone, and they had tar for mortar. And they said, 'Come, let us build ourselves a city, and a tower whose top will reach into heaven, and let us make for ourselves a name, lest we be scattered over the face of the whole earth.' Then Yahweh came down to see the city and the tower, which the sons of men had built. And Yahweh said, 'Behold, they are one people, and they have the same language. And this is what they have begun to do. So now nothing which they propose to do will be impossible for them. Come, let Us go down and there confuse their language, so that they will not understand one another's language.' So, Yahweh scattered them from there over the face of all the whole earth; and they stopped building the city. Therefore, its name was called Babel, because there Yahweh confused the language of the whole earth; and from there Yahweh scattered them over the face of all the whole earth." (Genesis 11:1–9)

⊤

Daleth

GABRIEL: Now that Yahweh had finished judging the earth with the flood, He established a new agreement with His surviving creation.

MICHAEL: And He promised that He would "never again strike down every living thing" as He did with the water of the flood (Genesis 8:21).

GABRIEL: He went on to guarantee stability: "While all the days of the earth remain, seedtime and harvest, and cold and heat, and summer and winter, and day and night shall not cease" (8:22).

MICHAEL: Some new parameters took place in that every creature would now fear and dread man.

GABRIEL: This was because man was also given every moving thing for food.

MICHAEL: This new covenant came into being between Yahweh and all His creatures.

GABRIEL: The sign given to verify this new agreement was a rainbow in the sky when the clouds rained.

MICHAEL: Yet it did not take man long to rebel against Yahweh, even after His commitment to them.

GABRIEL: Evil quickly surfaced again through one of Noah's sons. It came through his youngest son, Ham. Shem being the oldest and Japheth the second born.

MICHAEL: Let us go to Uriel and Raphael again to remind us as to what took place with Noah and his sons as they were very involved.

URIEL: Glad to be of service, most honorable Michael. Noah was not aware of the changes that took place with the flood.

RAPHAEL: Yes, now that the canopy over the earth had burst at the flood, the juice from the grape now fermented from the sun, and he unknowingly became drunk.

URIEL: I was amazed that this took place with this godly man but what followed resulted in far worse.

RAPHAEL: Many assumed that the sin of Ham was seeing his father naked in his tent. But "Seeing the nakedness" has a very specific meaning.

URIEL: Moses explains that Yahweh told Moses to announce to the people rules and statutes in order to not follow after the practices of people in Egypt and Canaan (Leviticus 18–20).

RAPHAEL: Yahweh said, "None of you shall approach any blood relative of his to uncover nakedness. I am Yahweh. You shall not uncover the nakedness of your father, that is, the nakedness of your mother. She is your mother; you are not to uncover her nakedness" (18:6–7).

URIEL: We read further that "if there is a man who lies with his father's wife, he has uncovered his father's nakedness" (20:11).

RAPHAEL: It is therefore clear that when Ham uncovered his father's nakedness, he was having sexual relations with his own mother while his father was drunk.

URIEL: This explains why when Noah woke from his wine, he knew immediately what his son had done against him.

RAPHAEL: Noah then cursed Canaan and not Ham because Canaan was the product of this unholy sexual union.

URIEL: Due to this curse, the descendants of Canaan were to be subservient to the other tribes.

RAPHAEL: And thus, tracking the family line of Ham provokes special interest.

URIEL: Particularly of note Ham's son Kush fathered Nimrod, who was the first on earth to be called "a mighty man."

RAPHAEL: He came to be called a mighty hunter before Yahweh, which does not carry a positive connotation, as we will discuss.

URIEL: Ham's, second son, Egypt, fathered a number of sons; however, the Casluhim (from whom came the Philistines) received special attention as it was from him the Philistines arose.

RAPHAEL: And Canaan produced the Jebusites, the Amorites, the Girgashites, and the Hivites, among others.

URIEL: As we know, these were evil people and often identified as being giants whom Israel battled for many years.

GABRIEL: So, obviously the Nephilim had been reestablished through possessing Ham and thus his descendants were hybrid demons.

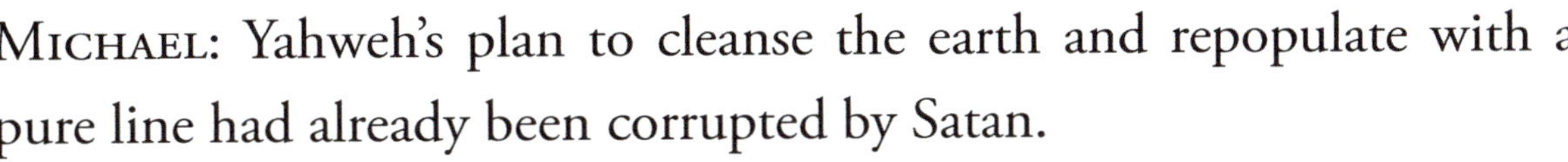

MICHAEL: Yahweh's plan to cleanse the earth and repopulate with a pure line had already been corrupted by Satan.

GABRIEL: And one such example had to be confronted immediately and that was Nimrod. Who began his kingdom in Babel and other cities in the land of Shinar.

MICHAEL: Rafael, give us your insight as you observed these events.

RAPHAEL: Well, at that time everyone spoke the same language, and instead of dispersing all over the earth as God had commanded, they congregated and migrated east to Shinar and settled there.

URIEL: Their leader, Nimrod, had an evil plan: "Come, let us build ourselves a city, and a tower whose top will reach into heavens, and let us make for ourselves a name, lest we be scattered over the face of the whole earth" (Genesis 11:4).

RAPHAEL: Henceforth the question arises: Where did Nimrod and his followers come up with the technology for bricks instead of stone and bitumen to replace mortar?

URIEL: From the same source as Cain's descendants who invented instruments of bronze, a skill too advanced for humans at that point in history. The unclean spirits were once again trying to stir up violence.

RAPHAEL: Yes, these are the metals used to forge weapons of warfare. And like the bricks, they were used in rebellion of our mighty King, Yahweh.

URIEL: I was shocked at the utter defiance of Nimrod and all the people. Although I should not have been since the reason Nimrod was so mighty resulted because he was another hybrid demon.

RAPHAEL: It was not long before Yahweh gave this effort a full inspection and concluded they would have no limits in what they could accomplish thereafter.

URIEL: No doubt Yahweh saw that this was man's effort to reach heaven on his own instead of depending on Him.

RAPHAEL: So, the Godhead, Yahweh, set a plan in place to thwart their rebellion. He would confuse their language, so they no longer understood each other.

URIEL: The result was what King Yahweh had intended from the beginning—the people separated from those they didn't understand and spread all over the face of the earth.

RAPHAEL: Each clan went to their designated part of the earth. Shem to the east and Japheth to the north and northwest.

URIEL: Ham for the most part went south and southwest. Consequently, the peoples of the earth migrated to the areas where they became identified.

GABRIEL: Satan's plan to disrupt Yahweh's intention had been foiled.

MICHAEL: Man had been forced to abide by Yahweh's command after all.

GABRIEL: And thus, we have the establishment of the various nations on earth.

"Now Cush was the father of Nimrod; he began to be a mighty one on the earth. He was a mighty hunter before Yahweh; therefore it is said, 'Like Nimrod a mighty hunter before Yahweh.' The beginning of his kingdom was Babel and Erech and Accad and Calneh, in the land of Shinar. From that land he went out to Assyria and built Nineveh and Rehoboth-Ir and Calah, and Resen between Nineveh and Calah; that is the great city. Mizraim was the father of Ludim and Anamim and Lehabim and Naphtuhim and Pathrusim and Casluhim (from whom came the Philistines) and Caphtorim. Now Cush was the father of Nimrod; he began to be a mighty one on the earth. He was a mighty hunter before Yahweh; therefore it is said,

'Like Nimrod a mighty hunter before Yahweh.' The beginning of his kingdom was Babel and Erech and Accad and Calneh, in the land of Shinar. From that land he went out to Assyria and built Nineveh and Rehoboth-Ir and Calah, and Resen between Nineveh and Calah; that is the great city. Mizraim was the father of Ludim and Anamim and Lehabim and Naphtuhim and Pathrusim and Casluhim (from whom came the Philistines) and Caphtorim." (Genesis 10:8–14)

CHAPTER 5

THE BELIEVING ABRAHAM

"And Yahweh said to Abram, 'Go forth from your land, and from your kin and from your father's house, to the land which I will show you; and I will make you a great nation, and I will bless you, and make your name great; and so you shall be a blessing; and I will bless those who bless you, and the one who curses you I will curse. And in you all the families of the earth will be blessed.' " (Genesis 12:1–3)

He

MICHAEL: As we continue examining angels' involvement in man's history, we trace the tribe of Shem until we reach Terah, who fathered Abram, Nahor, and Haran.

GABRIEL: And Terah migrated from Ur of the Chaldeans and went as far west as Haran and settled there.

MICHAEL: When Terah died, Yahweh called Abram to leave his country, kindred, and father's house to go to a land that He would show him.

GABRIEL: In conjunction with this move, Yahweh promised to make from him a great nation, bless him, and cause his name to be great. Through him Yahweh would bless all the families of the earth. (Genesis 12:1–3)

MICHAEL: Abram believed God, so he gathered all his possessions and set out for the land of Canaan.

GABRIEL: Even though the descendants of Canaan occupied that territory, Yahweh committed to give Abram and his offspring the entire area.

MICHAEL: Abram solidified his commitment in response to God's gift by worshiping at an altar he had built earlier to Yahweh near Bethel. (12:7)

GABRIEL: After Abram gave his nephew Lot the choice of the land, Yahweh reconfirmed His promises to Abram, and thus he built another altar in Hebron and worshipped Yahweh there. (Genesis 13:18)

MICHAEL: After many years, when there was still no evidence of a descendant, as was promised, Sarai and Abram decided to take the matter into their own hands.

GABRIEL: Yes, unwisely, Sarah gave her handmade Hagar to Abram as a wife. And when she quickly conceived, animosity developed between them. (Genesis 16:4)

MICHAEL: Due to Sarai's harsh dealing with Hagar, she fled into the wilderness.

GABRIEL: And this is where we meet the angel of Yahweh. So, in order for us to best recount the story, let's go to two of our fellow angels: Phanuel and Akhazriel.

PHANUEL: Thank you for the opportunity to help discuss these matters. As we know, when the Holy Scriptures use the name Yahweh, it refers to all three persons of the Godhead.

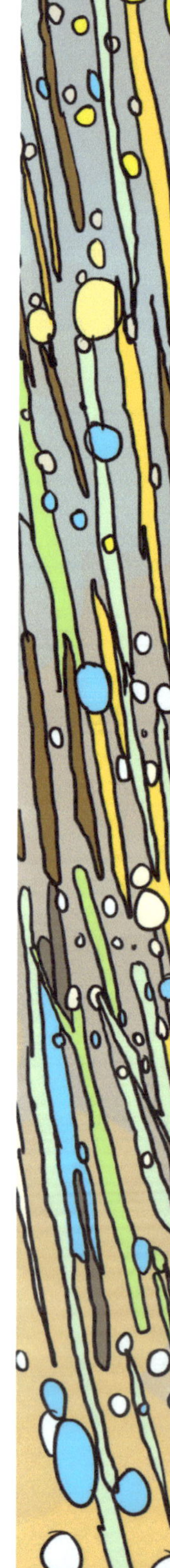

AKHAZRIEL: Many times, the individual persons of the Godhead are identified as the Father, the Son, and the Spirit. When the name *Yahweh* is used, it means the collective *we* or *us* of the Triunity.

PHANUEL: Consequently, the Angel of Yahweh does not just mean another one of us angels, as many tend to think. It has a very special connotation.

AKHAZRIEL: It is worth noting the distinction between *the* angel and *an* angel. *An* angel refers to any number of us. While *the* angel of Yahweh insinuates the second person of the Trinity—Jesus—is present.

PHANUEL: Multiple times it implies that the pre-incarnate Son of God has manifested Himself to humans. And since we know Jesus took on the form of a man at the incarnation, clearly, He shows Himself at these times as such.

AKHAZRIEL: Here with Hagar and later with Abram, He speaks as a man and looked like one as well. He gets right to the heart of the matter with several pointed questions for her.

PHANUEL: Then He seeks to console her while directing her and goes on to prophesy about the great nation that would come through her. (16:10)

AKHAZRIEL: At this point she realizes it is Yahweh Himself in human form she is dealing with and acknowledges how He looks after her.

MICHAEL: Thank you two for this recollection of these events. Now let us consider the next interaction of Abram with our brethren through Amaliel and Barattiel, who were eyewitnesses.

AMALIEL: We angels connected with Abram, now called Abraham, and his nephew Lot in association with the towns of Sodom and Gomorrah.

BARATTIEL: At that time Yahweh, in the person of Jesus Himself, manifested along with Amaliel and myself. Here we appeared as men to them.

AMALIEL: Abraham realized right away that we were not just any ordinary men when we approached his tent, and he insisted we accept his offer of hospitality. (Genesis 18:1–5)

BARATTIEL: When Abraham understood we were there to judge the cities for their immorality, he pleaded for longsuffering by Yahweh. (18:24–32)

AMALIEL: And while Jesus remained in Abraham's presence, we arrived in Sodom and were greeted by Lot. He made every effort to convince us not to stay overnight in the town square for our protection. (Genesis 19:2)

BARATTIEL: It was disturbing to me that the townspeople forced their perverse sexual agenda upon us. And we pulled Lot inside his house for refuge and blinded the pursuers to end their assault. (19:10–11)

AMALIEL: The following day we pressed Lot, his wife, and daughters to flee to the hills, and subsequently we initiated the judgement of God with fire and brimstone. (19:15)

BARATTIEL: We warned them not to look back at the destruction. But Lot's wife refused to listen and was promptly turned into a pillar of salt which was just but hard for Lot to handle. (19:26)

AMALIEL: Lot and his daughters were quickly ushered away to safety in the nearby hills, and thus our service to Yahweh was fulfilled with regard to this mission.

GABRIEL: Thank you both for this eyewitness account. It is always good to hear the story first hand.

MICHAEL: And so, we have discussed our primary encounters with Abraham whose gift of faith was counted as righteousness.

GABRIEL: Yahweh's holiness and justice are always balanced with His faithfulness and grace. Extol the name of the King over all!

"Then Yahweh appeared to him by the oaks of Mamre, while he was sitting at the tent door in the heat of the day. And he lifted up his eyes and looked, and behold, three men were standing nearby; he saw, and he ran from the tent door to meet them, and he bowed himself to the earth, and he said, 'My Lord, if now I have found favor in Your sight, please do not pass Your servant by. Please let a little water be brought and wash your feet, and rest yourselves under the tree; and let me bring a piece of bread, that you may refresh your hearts; after that you may pass on, since in such a manner you have passed by your servant.' And they said, 'So you shall do, as you have said.' " (Genesis 18:1–5)

CHAPTER 6

THE LAUGHING ISAAC

"Now Yahweh visited Sarah as He had said, and Yahweh did for Sarah as He had promised. So Sarah conceived and bore a son to Abraham in his old age, at the appointed time of which God had spoken to him. And Abraham called the name of his son who was born to him, whom Sarah bore to him, Isaac." (Genesis 21:1–3)

Vav

MICHAEL: It came to pass when Abraham had his own heir through Sarah, he was named Isaac, which means, "he laughs." The laughter refers to both Abraham and Sarah's comical response to Yahweh's pledge to fulfill His promise of a son.

GABRIEL: So Saragael, tell us the story of what followed when Isaac had grown up.

SARAGAEL: Pleased to recount my part in this piece of history as our King had summoned my service in this intervention.

MICHAEL: What happened to initiate this encounter?

SARAGAEL: Our Master revealed to Abraham that he was not to take a wife for his son from among the Canaanites, who were not a holy people.

GABRIEL: No, they were a cursed tribe who were mixed with fallen angels.

SARAGAEL: Therefore, Abraham instructed his servant to journey to his kindred in Haran to take a wife for his son. (Genesis 24:4)

MICHAEL: It seems that his servant had some reluctance and asked about his options if he was not successful in bringing a bride back.

Saragael: Abraham most vehemently opposed taking his son back to Nahor in Mesopotamia. This was due to Yahweh guiding him to the land He had promised Abraham and his family.

Gabriel: How did our Maker reassure the servant that his mission would be successful?

Saragael: He had Abraham instruct his servant that I would go before him to prepare the way for its completion. Not only would I guide him as to the path to follow, but also arrange everything with Abraham's kindred.

Michael: Describe the way their process developed.

Saragael: Abraham made his servant swear an oath before Yahweh that he would do exactly as he was instructed. Then the servant equipped ten of his master's camels with choice gifts and proceeded to the family in Mesopotamia. (24:9–10)

Gabriel: What did he do when he arrived there?

Saragael: He posed the camels by the water well in the evening when women go there to draw water. The servant then prayed to Yahweh that He would grant success in this quest. (24:12)

MICHAEL: Did he ask specifically how this would take place?

SARAGAEL: Very much so. He asked that the young woman whom he asked for a drink, say yes and offer to water his camels also. He asked that this one would be God's appointed wife for Isaac and thus show steadfast love to his master. (24:14)

GABRIEL: And did this quickly come to pass?

SARAGAEL: Before he even finished uttering his prayer, Rebekah came out with her water jar and filled it at the spring. And when the servant asked her for a drink, she quickly lowered her jar and gave him some water. When he had drunk, she offered to supply water for all the camels as well! (24:19)

MICHAEL: And what was the servant thinking as this took place?

SARAGAEL: He was waiting on Yahweh to learn whether his journey had prospered, and when she completed the watering, he brought out a gold ring and bracelets for her. Then he asked her whose daughter she was and if there was room for them to spend the night. (24:22–23)

GABRIEL: How did she respond to these questions?

SARAGAEL: She replied she was Nahor's descendant and that there was plenty of room and food for everyone. The servant then bowed his head and worshipped Yahweh. (24:24–26)

MICHAEL: How did her family react when Rebecca filled them in?

SARAGAEL: She went with excitement to tell her household, and her brother Laban got involved personally when he saw the ring and the bracelets along with her explanation.

GABRIEL: What did Laban do in response?

SARAGAEL: He ran to the servant and encouraged him to come enjoy their hospitality prepared for them. The servant then followed him, and all agreed to the refreshment, except he would not allow himself to eat just yet. (24:31–33)

MICHAEL: What was his reason for refusing to partake?

SARAGAEL: The servant would not permit himself this satisfaction until he completed his master Abraham's business. Thus, he went through all the events leading up to this encounter with Laban and family.

GABRIEL: What kinds of information did he disclose?

SARAGAEL: He filled them in on how Yahweh had prospered Abraham from the time he had left Haran. Then he went on to tell of Isaacs' miraculous birth in their old age. (24:36)

MICHAEL: How did the servant link Isaac and the trip to Haran?

SARAGAEL: He related how Abraham did not want to choose a wife for him from the people of the land and made him swear to seek Isaac's spouse for him from his kinsman. And when he was questioned about what to do if he was not successful, he related how an angel (me) would lead the way and prepare the circumstances. (24:37–41)

GABRIEL: How did he convey how Yahweh carried this out?

SARAGAEL: He shared his specific prayer to Yahweh and how He fulfilled it in every detail. When he determined that he had been led to Abraham's family, he gave his gifts to Rebecca and bowed in worship for the incredible manifestation. (24:48)

MICHAEL: What was his next request?

SARAGAEL: In a straightforward manner, he asked for an answer to his dilemma. Either Rebecca would become Isaac's bride or she would not. With this finality, he would know his next steps. (24:49)

GABRIEL: How did Laban and his mother respond?

SARAGAEL: They quickly surmised that if this plan was from Yahweh, then how could they refuse. They gave permission for the servant to take Rebecca to be Isaac's wife according to God's direction. (24:50–51)

MICHAEL: Was this the final resolution of the matter?

SARAGAEL: Well, not completely. The positive response caused Abraham's servant to once more bow and worship to Yahweh. Then he gave out jewelry and costly garments to all. With this, he and his men finally ate and drank before spending the night. (24:52–53)

GABRIEL: How did it go when it came time to leave in the morning?

SARAGAEL: When he asked to be sent away back to this master along with the young woman, her family asked that Rebecca be allowed to wait a few days before going. (24:55)

MICHAEL: What did the servant say to this objection?

SARAGAEL: He requested that they not delay him from returning to his master, now that Yahweh had prospered his way. To which they called Rebecca and asked if she was willing to go with them now. (24:58)

GABRIEL: And her reply, we can all guess.

SARAGAEL: Of course, she was willing to go, and so they sent her and her handmaiden off with their blessing to go with the servant and his men on the journey to Isaac in the Negev. (24:59)

MICHAEL: Describe the long-awaited meeting between Isaac and Rebekah.

SARAGAEL: What a beautiful picture this was! Isaac was out praying in the field when the camel train arrived with Rebekah in tow.

MICHAEL: How did this story conclude?

SARAGAEL: When she noticed him, she dismounted and asked who the man was. When the servant confirmed that he was his master's son, Isaac, she veiled her face. (24:65)

GABRIEL: What did Isaac do?

SARAGAEL: As they appeared on the horizon, Isaac moved toward them with anticipation. He gazed at her charms intently while the servant explained everything that had taken place.

MICHAEL: Finally, describe how this quest concluded.

SARAGAEL: After exchanging pleasantries, they quickly bonded to each other. They were thrilled over their newfound romance and were pleased at this long-desired meeting.

SARAGAEL: When Rebecca had freshened up from her travels, as you would expect, Isaac brought her into his mother's tent and took her as his wife and loved her dearly. (24:67)

MICHAEL: Did this have a good effect on him after his mother's death?

SARAGAEL: Oh, yes. This marriage brought deep consolation to Isaac's grieving heart. Their love became a means for staying grounded throughout their many days together in this life.

GABRIEL: What a satisfying story to relive! Thank you, Saragael, for this detailed depiction.

MICHAEL: It is supremely rewarding to see how the Almighty uses us to accomplish many tasks and help bring beautiful consequences of the relationships.

GABRIEL: It is always a pleasure to bring joy to our great King's heart!

"Now Abraham was old, advanced in age; and Yahweh had blessed Abraham in every way. And Abraham said to his servant, the oldest of his household, who ruled over all that he owned, "Please place your hand under my thigh, and I will make you swear by Yahweh, the God of heaven and the God of earth, that you shall not take a wife for my son from the daughters of the Canaanites, among whom I live, but you will go to my land and to my kin, and take a wife for my son Isaac." And the servant said to him, "Suppose the woman is not willing to follow me to this land; should I indeed take your son back to the land from where you came?" Then Abraham said to him, "Beware lest you take my son back there! Yahweh, the God of heaven, who took me from my father's house and from the land of my kin, and who spoke to me and who swore to me, saying, 'To your seed I will give this land,' He will send His angel before you, and you will take a wife for my son from there. But if the woman is not willing to follow you, then you will be free from this oath of mine; only do not take my son back there." So the servant placed his hand under the thigh of Abraham his master and swore to him concerning this matter." (Genesis 24:1–9)

CHAPTER 7

THE CONNIVING JACOB

"Then Jacob departed from Beersheba and went toward Haran. And he reached a certain place and spent the night there because the sun had set; and he took one of the stones of the place and put it under his head and lay down in that place. Then he had a dream, and behold, a ladder stood on the earth with its top touching heaven; and behold, the angels of God were ascending and descending on it. . . .

"Then Jacob awoke from his sleep and said, 'Surely Yahweh is in this place, and I did not know it.' And he was afraid and said, 'How fearsome is this place! This is none other than the house of God, and this is the gate of heaven.'

"So Jacob rose early in the morning and took the stone that he had put under his head and set it up as a pillar and poured oil on its top. And he called the name of that place Bethel; however, previously the name of the city had been Luz." (Genesis 28:10–12, 16–19)

ℸ

Zayin

MICHAEL: The next time we interacted with men was when Rebecca's twins, Esau and Jacob, were adults.

GABRIEL: Up to that point, Jacob had lived up to his name, which means "supplanter" as he deceived his way to receiving both Esau's birthright and blessing.

MICHAEL: Therefore, out of fear and because he wanted to please his parents, Jacob went to Haran, to their kindred Laban.

GABRIEL: But to get a first-hand testimony about what took place along the way, let us hear from Camiel who was witness to these events.

CAMIEL: As Jacob journeyed north, he had a vision in the night where he saw angels ascending and descending on a stairway between earth and heaven. (Genesis 28:12)

MICHAEL: That is rather humorous as there are a multitude of avenues connecting heaven and earth, and Yahweh had just revealed to him one such spot.

CAMIEL: The great King Yahweh spoke to him directly from the top of the stairs, affirming that if Jacob returned to Canaan, He would fulfill His promise to give him the land obligated to his forefathers. (28:15)

GABRIEL: This must have made quite an impression on young Jacob.

CAMIEL: When he awoke, at first he realized that Yahweh had been in that place, and he did not know it (v 16). This irony is that Yahweh is in every place and people just are not aware of it.

MICHAEL: How did Jacob express his appreciation for Yahweh's affirmation of His promise?

CAMIEL: Jacob used the rock on which he had been sleeping as an altar to worship Yahweh. He poured oil on it and asserted that if Yahweh accompanies him and will protect him, He will be his God forever. (28:18)

GABRIEL: How did Yahweh prosper Jacob in his efforts?

CAMIEL: Yahweh led him to the well where Leban's daughter Rachel brought their sheep to be watered. And when he revealed he was the son of Rebecca, Laban's sister, Rachel ran back to tell her father. (Genesis 29:12)

MICHAEL: Did Laban respond favorably?

CAMIEL: He fully embraced him and invited him to his house where Jacob shared the whole story with his kindred. In exuberance, Laban

affirmed their relationship and consequently, Jacob stayed with them for a lengthy time. (29:14)

GABRIEL: What were the arrangements they made?

CAMIEL: Jacob would work for seven years as wages for Rachel, his younger daughter, whom Jacob preferred over Leah, the older. This length of service seemed minimal to him because of his great love for her. (29:20)

MICHAEL: Did Laban follow through with his promise to Jacob?

CAMIEL: He deceived Jacob by switching his daughters on the wedding night. And, of course, Jacob was incensed that he would trick him this way. Laban then defended his actions as the oldest was always given in marriage before the younger in their culture. (29:26)

GABRIEL: How did they work out this deadlock?

CAMIEL: Laban agreed that Jacob could also marry Rachel after Leah's wedding week if he would work another seven years for her. So, after completing Leah's week, he married Rachel, whom he loved most. (29:28)

MICHAEL: Describe the way having multiple wives worked out for Jacob?

CAMIEL: Immediately a competition arose between the sisters to prove who was the more valuable by how many children they each bore to Jacob. And Yahweh prospered Leah in this maybe to make up for not being loved as much.

GABRIEL: In what ways did both Leah and Rachel demonstrate ungodly attitudes?

CAMIEL: It was clear that Leah believed her performance would win over her husband. She clearly had an identity problem, not believing she was enough. While Rachel showed her lack of trust in Yahweh and depended on her own efforts of coercion. (Genesis 30:1)

MICHAEL: How was Jacob affected by this dissension?

CAMIEL: Jacob could feel the extra pressure put upon him, and it angered him. He made a wise declaration when he asked if he were in "the place of God who has withheld from you the fruit of the womb?" (30:2)

GABRIEL: What was Rachel's next step in this drama?

CAMIEL: Like her predecessor Sarah, she offered her servant, Bilhah, as a surrogate, and when Jacob went into her, she conceived. This resulted in a son and then a second as well.

MICHAEL: What perspective did Rachel convey with this development?

CAMIEL: She believed God had finally listened to her and that she had wrestled with her sister and come out on top. (30:8)

GABRIEL: Did this end their conflict?

CAMIEL: No. Leah continued the feud by also offering her maid Zilpah to Jacob as another wife. Wow, the situation just became busier and crazier as Zilpah also bore Jacob two more sons. (30:12)

MICHAEL: To what depths did these two go?

CAMIEL: They even went to the extent of bargaining for Jacob's affection. Leah exchanged her son's mandrakes for a night with Jacob. Jacob must have been amazed when Leah approached him that evening and let him know how she had gained privileges with him after offering Rachel food. (30:16)

GABRIEL: What were the repercussions of this episode?

CAMIEL: Leah was allowed to bear Jacob two more sons, and consequently she concluded that now her husband would honor her—still trying to win his approval by providing him six sons. (30:19)

MICHAEL: Was master Yahweh finished with Rachel at this point?

CAMIEL: No, He called her to mind and listened to her pleas, opening her womb and producing a son, Joseph. She then felt like God had taken away her stigma. (30:24)

GABRIEL: What did Jacob do then?

CAMIEL: He asked for Laban to send him away with all his family to his own country. Laban knew he prospered because of Yahweh's blessing on Jacob. Consequently, they began to negotiate as to what it would take for him to stay. (30:27–31)

MICHAEL: Were they able to settle this peacefully?

CAMIEL: Not a chance since neither of them trusted each other. When they implemented a plan, Jacob came out ahead. This brought accusations by Laban's sons about Jacob swindling his wealth, and so Jacob promptly fled. Yahweh confirmed he should now go back to his homeland and promised to be with him in this. (Genesis 31:13)

GABRIEL: How did Jacob's wives respond to this decision?

CAMIEL: In unison they recognized that their father had, in effect, sold them for his own profit and that there would be no inheritance from him. Therefore, they encouraged Jacob to do as God had directed him. (31:14–16)

MICHAEL: What then did Jacob do in response?

CAMIEL: He gathered all his possessions in haste and headed for his homeland. But just to spice up the situation further, Rachel meanwhile stole her father's idols while he was shearing his sheep. (31:19)

GABRIEL: When did Laban figure out he had been tricked?

CAMIEL: It took a couple of days before he was told that Jacob had fled, but then he hotly pursued them and closed the distance. (31:23)

MICHAEL: Was there a comment from the Almighty about these events?

CAMIEL: Absolutely, Yahweh came to Laban in a dream and told him to be careful not to speak to Jacob, either good or bad, and thus the conversation between the two was tempered when he caught up. But Laban still questioned Jacob as to why he had acted thusly. (31:26–28)

GABRIEL: I'm sure Laban had much to say to Jacob, right?

CAMIEL: Yes, Laban hid behind his pretense to only wanting to give them a fond farewell. Then he turned around and accused Jacob of stealing his household idols. (31:30)

MICHAEL: What was Jacob's response to Laban's contentions?

CAMIEL: He vehemently denied that there was any truth in these comments and declared if they found anything in their possession, the person responsible would die—not realizing Rachel had done this. (31:32)

GABRIEL: So how was Rachel not caught in this trespass?

CAMIEL: She used a bit of her own deceit by hiding the idols in her saddle and sitting on them saying she couldn't come down due to it being her time of the month. (31:35)

MICHAEL: Did Jacob handle all this well?

CAMIEL: No, he now used this occasion as an excuse for berating Laban for all his mistreatment toward him. He brought up ten times Laban had changed his wages over the last twenty years. He swore he had never done Laban any wrong and that if it wasn't for Yahweh watching out for him, he would have left empty handed. (31:41–42)

GABRIEL: What was Leban's response to all these declarations?

CAMIEL: He stated that everything that Jacob owned had all come from him, yet for the good of his daughters and grandchildren, he suggested they make a truce. (31:43–44)

MICHAEL: In what way did they initiate this covenant?

CAMIEL: They gathered stones and considered this heap to be a witness between them, that they would each do right by the other and not cross this boundary to harm each other. They asked that Yahweh, the God of their fathers, judge between them. (31:45–53)

GABRIEL: Did they then part in peace?

CAMIEL: Laban arose the next morning, kissed his grandchildren and daughters, blessed them and returned to his home. (31:55)

MICHAEL: Now you might think Jacob could just settle into a peaceful way of life, right?

CAMIEL: Jacob certainly had been through enough hardship already, but now our King had more in mind for him to learn. Just in case you forgot, he had some issues with his brother to settle as well.

GABRIEL: How did Jacob approach this impending conflict?

CAMIEL: To fully describe this continuing story, I've asked several of the other angels who witnessed these events to be a part of this conversation. Welcome, Erelin, Hadramiel, and Jael!

ERELIN: Pleased to contribute to this important review of our involvement with humans. As Jacob departed from Gilead, we met him to give him support in a place he named Mahanaim, or God's camp. (Genesis 32:1–2)

MICHAEL: I'm sure you gave him instruction as to how to deal with Esau, right?

HADRAMIEL: Jacob followed our directions explicitly and sent messengers ahead to prepare Esau for his return and all his entourage. When they returned, they reported that Esau was coming out to meet him. (32:6)

GABRIEL: I think we all know Jacob's tendencies when presented with threatening circumstances. Did he come through true to form?

JAEL: He was afraid of the four hundred men accompanying Esau, and therefore he divided up his people and flocks. Thus, he attempted to reduce his losses if they attacked and at least some would escape alive. (32:7)

MICHAEL: Jacob did tend to always consider the worst that may come.

ERELIN: In view of the impending doom, Jacob surprised us all by humbling himself before Yahweh. He admitted he wasn't worthy of all the loyal love and favor that he had been shown. (32:10)

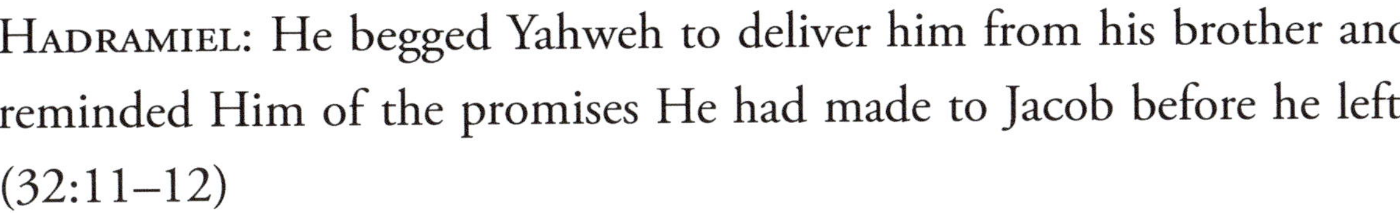

HADRAMIEL: He begged Yahweh to deliver him from his brother and reminded Him of the promises He had made to Jacob before he left. (32:11–12)

JAEL: Even still, he made plans to try to appease his brother, sending livestock ahead as a present in several droves while indicating he would be following behind. (32:13–16)

GABRIEL: What did Jacob do next?

HADRAMIEL: He sent his wives, servants, children, and all that he had across the ford of the Jabbok, but he remained alone. (32:22–23)

JAEL: Then I wrestled with him and he sought God's favor thinking I was God Himself. Jacob fought so violently that I had to touch his hip to put it out of socket. Even then he didn't relent and said he wouldn't stop until I blessed him and told him my name. (32:24–27)

ERELIN: You didn't give him your name, but you were given permission to change his name to Israel since he had striven with God's representative and prevailed.

MICHAEL: Obviously this blessing was key for Jacob to obtain since he was about to meet his brother and was unsure of the outcome of that meeting.

HADRAMIEL: Yes, Jacob (now Israel) could face this dilemma even though he would do so with a limp from his hip injury.

GABRIEL: Yahweh had thus given Jacob the assurance to face the danger which lay ahead of him.

JAEL: When Jacob saw Esau and his men approaching, he staged his family from the least first to the greatest at the last, but it was all for naught because Esau ran to greet Jacob, hugged him, and kissed him as they wept together. (Genesis 33:1–4)

ERELIN: Then Esau questioned him about the preceding company and the gifts offered. Jacob told him it was to seek his favor, and he finally convinced him to accept the gifts. (33:11)

HADRAMIEL: I also think part of Jacob's reasoning was to show that he had changed from being deceptive and greedy to honest and generous. He earnestly sought Esau's forgiveness for his transgressions.

MICHAEL: Therefore, as we know, they parted in peace and Jacob returned to the area where his grandfather and father had dwelt. And there in Shechem and in Bethel Yahweh instructed him to build an altar to Him. (33:18–20)

Erelin: Exactly, this was the precise place where King Yahweh appeared to Jacob before he fled to Padam-Aram.

Jael: And He confirmed his name change from Jacob ("deceiver") to Israel ("he who strives with God"). (Genesis 35:10)

Hadramiel: He also reaffirmed His covenant with Abraham's lineage and the promise Jacob would inherit this land along with his offspring. (35:12)

Gabriel: And we know that Rachel died giving birth to a son—Benjamin—as they journeyed toward Bethlehem. (35:18)

Michael: Then, after burying her, Jacob went to his father's house in Hebron. And soon after, Isaac's days were completed and so his sons buried him there. (35:29)

Gabriel: Israel and his twelve sons prospered until the day when the brothers out of envy sold Joseph into slavery in Egypt. (Genesis 37:28)

Michael: Israel grieved many days over the loss of his favorite son who ended up being sold to one of Pharaohs officers. Yet Joseph prospered in every way regardless of the circumstances.

Gabriel: Yahweh even raised Joseph up to second in command in Egypt! (Genesis 41:37–43)

MICHAEL: The Almighty's wisdom began to unfold when there was a devastating famine and Israel and his sons had nowhere else to go but Egypt.

GABRIEL: Providentially, Joseph had ordered the storing of the net grain for which Egypt had become wealthy. (41:49)

MICHAEL: When Joseph demanded that the brothers bring their father, Israel was reluctant to go, but Yahweh reassured him that He would go with him to Egypt. (Genesis 46:3)

GABRIEL: And so, with many tears, the entire family was reunited once Joseph revealed his identity.

MICHAEL: When Israel's final days approached, he called all his sons together and blessed them with predictions of their future. (Genesis 49:1–27)

GABRIEL: With the completion of this task and the promise that he would be taken back to be buried with his family, Israel pulled himself up into his bed and breathed his last. (49:33)

MICHAEL: Thus, with much fanfare, Joseph and his brothers with a great entourage of Egyptian elders and servants fulfilled their promise to bury Israel back in the land of Canaan. (Genesis 50:7–9)

GABRIEL: So concluded the 147 years of Israel (Jacob) son of Isaac, son of Abraham, and the multitude of adventures we lived out with them.

MICHAEL: Thank you to all of you fellow angels for your wonderful explanations of the events related to Jacob (Israel). This sure fills in so much more of the story.

"And he [Jacob] blessed Joseph and said, 'May the God before whom my fathers Abraham and Isaac walked, the God who has been my shepherd throughout my life to this day, the angel who has redeemed me from all evil, bless these boys; and may my name live on in them, and the names of my fathers Abraham and Isaac; and may they grow into a multitude in the midst of the earth.' "
(Genesis. 48:15–16)

CHAPTER 8

THE COMMANDING MOSES

"Behold, I am going to send an angel before you to keep you along the way and to bring you into the place which I have prepared. Keep watch of yourself before him and listen to his voice; do not be rebellious toward him, for he will not pardon your transgression, since My name is in him. But if you truly listen to his voice and do all that I speak, then I will be an enemy to your enemies and an adversary to your adversaries. For My angel will go before you and bring you in to the land of the Amorites, the Hittites, the Perizzites, the Canaanites, the Hivites, and the Jebusites; and I will annihilate them." (Exodus 23:20–23)

Heth

MICHAEL: Now after Joseph and his brothers died, there arose a new ruler in Egypt who did not know Joseph nor of the benefits he had brought to Egypt. (Exodus 1:8)

GABRIEL: The new Pharoah was afraid of the sons of Israel because they were great in number and might, so he designed plans to keep them in subjectivity. (1:9)

MICHAEL: Therefore, he multiplied the difficulty of their labor so that the people moaned and cried out to Yahweh for relief.

GABRIEL: It was then that King Yahweh provided a deliverer from His people. This one—Moses—was raised by Pharaoh's daughter as her own. (Exodus 2:9)

MICHAEL: After he fled for killing an Egyptian and established his life as a shepherd to his father-in-law's flocks, then Yahweh revealed Himself to him. (Exodus 3:2)

GABRIEL: When Yahweh asked him to bring his people out of bondage, Moses requested to know the name of this God of their fathers, so he would have credibility with the people. (3:13)

MICHAEL: Then Yahweh explained not only what His Name is, but also all that it means—giving Moses confidence. It always helps to know more about your god.

GABRIEL: Yes, all that the King embodies has been conveyed through His name for all generations. He has been, is, and always will be faithful, unchanging, everywhere-present, self-existent, all-knowing, all-wise, always wanting the best for His creatures.

MICHAEL: Consequently, it is no wonder that this name is how He wishes to be known. Even the name Jesus bears these qualities since Jeshua means "Yahweh saves."

GABRIEL: Thus, with the power of the name and all it entails, Moses was willing to carry out King Yahweh's directives.

MICHAEL: Exactly, Yahweh understood Moses' frailties, so He supplied Aaron, his brother, to speak on his behalf and gave him the ability to perform many signs and judgments through his staff. (Exodus 4)

GABRIEL: After much travail and many plagues, Pharaoh would promise to relinquish the people of Israel, only to harden his heart after finding relief. (Exodus 7–10)

MICHAEL: But with the final judgment of death to the first born, this seemed to disturb Pharaoh enough to let them go. (Exodus 12:29–32)

GABRIEL: Very true! However, as soon as they were leaving, Pharaoh changed his mind and with his army pursued them to the sea. (Exodus 14:5–8)

MICHAEL: And just when the host of Israel seemed trapped, Yahweh performed another miracle. He opened the Red Sea for His people yet closed it over the Egyptians to their demise. (14:21–29)

GABRIEL: With much complaining, Israel was led through the wilderness, even rebellion against their commander. Nevertheless, Yahweh showed much long-suffering toward them.

MICHAEL: And here another of our host comes to continue the story. Kezef please fill us in on your insight at this point.

KEZEF: Yahweh told me to lead His people to the promised land. I was chosen to lead them to victory over the various tribes in Canaan.

GABRIEL: How did the great Yahweh direct them to follow you? Were the people of Israel responsive to your leadership?

KEZEF: He told them I would go before them to guard them on the way and that I would bring them to the land. They were instructed to pay attention to my words of direction and obey them. (Exodus 33:2)

MICHAEL: What warning did our Most High give them about rebelling?

KEZEF: They were made aware that, unlike Yahweh, I would not pardon their transgressions against me.

GABRIEL: Describe the promises offered if they did obey your voice.

KEZEF: If they carefully followed my commands, then Yahweh would be their ally and blot out all their enemies in Canaan.

MICHAEL: What was the process before they set out on their journey?

KEZEF: Moses was called up to the mountain where Yahweh's presence dwelt in the cloud covering it. There Yahweh instructed Moses as to all aspects of the tabernacle where Israel was to worship. (Exodus 26–31)

GABRIEL: Were they given detailed explanation of how they were to function?

KEZEF: Moses wrote down all these directives from Yahweh as to how they were to conduct worship, and finally he received the ten commandments, written by the finger of God Himself on stone tablets.

MICHAEL: How was Moses received by the people when he returned after forty days on the mountain with the glory of Yahweh?

KEZEF: The people had grown impatient and determined to fashion a golden calf for themselves to worship. This substitution was met with wrath both by Yahweh and His servant Moses.

GABRIEL: Give us the details as to how Moses dealt with their rebellion.

KEZEF: After Moses cast down the tablets to their destruction, he burned the golden calf to powder and scattered it into the people's water and made them drink it. (Exodus 32:20)

MICHAEL: What repercussions did the people endure for this treachery?

KEZEF: Moses called the Levites to his side, and they followed his command to kill many of the throng then Yahweh sent a plague among the people so that many more were destroyed. (32:27, 35)

GABRIEL: So then describe Moses' recourse with King Yahweh after this event.

KEZEF: He sought to atone for Israel's great transgression by interceding on their behalf in the tent of meeting where Yahweh would speak with him face to face. Moses refused to lead the people into battle with the inhabitants of Canaan, unless Yahweh would go with them. (Exodus 33:14)

MICHAEL: Yahweh demonstrated grace for the people because of the favor He had for Moses and then He revealed the perfection of His glory to him.

GABRIEL: Although, as angels, we are accustomed to seeing Him in this manner, this must have been revolutionary for Moses to see.

KEZEF: Undeniably true! Then Yahweh instructed him to come back to the mountain and there, He wrote again the commandments on more stone tablets. (Exodus 34:1)

MICHAEL: How did the people respond the second time Moses came down from the mountain?

KEZEF: The people were at that point given a responsive heart to bring about the work of the tabernacle according to Yahweh's instructions. (Exodus 35:22)

GABRIEL: With these designations fulfilled, how did the multitude move forward toward entering the Promised Land?

KEZEF: From the day of the tabernacle's completion, the glory of Yahweh filled the tent with a cloud. And whenever the cloud of His glory moved from above the tabernacle, the people of Israel would set out.

MICHAEL: Did this vary from the nighttime?

KEZEF: The cloud would lead them by day and a pillar of fire preceded them by night and in this way they proceeded throughout the years of their journey in the wilderness. (Exodus 40:34–38)

GABRIEL: It is apparent that when they arrived at the borders of the land, they rejected the good scout's report and would not believe Yahweh that they would be victorious over the giants in the land. (Numbers 13:32–33)

KEZEF: And thus, they were sentenced to forty more years of wandering in the wilderness. It would be until that generation died off before the nation would be allowed to enter the land.

MICHAEL: Such a sad report that they did not trust our King to bring them the victory and cleanse the land from the inhabitants who would tempt them to worship their false gods.

KEZEF: Regretfully Moses was faced with dealing with a stiff-necked and rebellious generation through those many years of punishment, until the time came for the new descendants to be led into taking over the Promised Land.

GABRIEL: The second time, the people were responsive and followed the directions of Yahweh to fight their enemies and inherit the land. (Deuteronomy 3)

MICHAEL: And yet they did not even then fully follow Yahweh's directives since they didn't fully cleanse the land completely of its evil people.

"But now go, guide the people where I told you. Behold, My angel shall go before you; nevertheless in the day when I punish, I will punish them for their sin." (Exodus 32:34)

CHAPTER 9

THE DELIGHTING DAVID

"But now [Saul's] kingdom shall not endure. Yahweh has sought out for Himself a man after His own heart, and Yahweh has appointed him as ruler over His people because you have not kept what Yahweh commanded you." (1 Samuel 13:14)

Teth

MICHAEL: Now our pilgrimage moves ahead from a prophet and priest of sorts in Moses to hundreds of years later to a godly king in David.

GABRIEL: Joshua took over after Moses' death, and he, along with many valiant warriors, fought with the evil Canaanites who were giants since they were hybrid demons.

MICHAEL: But King Yahweh's directions to totally destroy these inhabitants were not completely followed. (Judges 1:27–28)

GABRIEL: And the peoples of Israel reaped the consequences of their lack of devotion. They strayed to worship the false gods of the land as foretold.

MICHAEL: The Most High gave them judges to rescue them from their judgment, and time after time they obeyed briefly and then resorted to their unfaithfulness.

GABRIEL: It seemed they never fully learned their lesson, and Yahweh repeatedly brought the judgment as promised.

MICHAEL: Eventually they complained they wanted a king to rule over them like the nations surrounding them, not wanting Yahweh to be their king as intended. (1 Samuel 8:6)

GABRIEL: And so, He relented, and let them have a king, Saul, who led them inconsistently at best. Ultimately losing his mind, he was overcome by demons and ended up taking his own life.

MICHAEL: There is no better example of this tragedy than when Saul sought to kill the new heir to the throne, the anointed one, King David.

GABRIEL: David grew from obscurity to great favor when, as a youth, he took down the Philistines' champion giant, Goliath, after he defamed the Most High before Israel's army. (1 Samuel 17:31–54)

MICHAEL: Yahweh raised David up despite Saul's attempts to destroy him, and even Jonathan, Saul's son, helped rescue him. (1 Samuel 18:3)

GABRIEL: After Saul was rejected as king, during battle he was wounded and then he took his own life (1 Samuel 31:4). Consequently, David was crowned the rightful ruler and Israel prospered under his leadership. (2 Samuel 2:7)

MICHAEL: David did have an incident where when enticed by Satan, he pushed to number the people. (2 Samuel 24:1)

GABRIEL: Even when Joab, the commander of his armies and a cousin, confronted David with the error of this direction, David forged ahead. (2 Samuel 24:3)

MICHAEL: This action conveyed a dependence on the flesh instead of the Spirit of the Holy One. Like the time when David gave into his lustful desires toward Bathsheba.

GABRIEL: It had never been about self-reliance and the sheer numbers of the people of Israel.

MICHAEL: The reason Abraham, Isaac, and Israel had been successful was entirely due to Yahweh and His intervention to protect and rescue them.

GABRIEL: The exodus from Egypt is a perfect example of how Yahweh made a way for Israel to leave and defended them in doing so.

MICHAEL: Yahweh had sustained them through forty years in the wilderness and then gave them success in battle over Canaan.

GABRIEL: Time and time again the merciful King had supplied a way to escape destruction.

MICHAEL: And now because David was depending on Israel's own strength, Yahweh gave him the choice of three punishments.

GABRIEL: Gad, David's seer, delivered the message that he could either endure three years of famine, three months of destruction by foes, or three days of pestilence from the angel of Yahweh. (24:13)

MICHAEL: David realized his great error and decided to put Israel in the hand of Yahweh who might be merciful.

GABRIEL: And so, Yahweh sent Kezef to carry out the destruction in the land, until seventy thousand succumbed. (24:15)

MICHAEL: Finally, the angel of Yahweh—Jesus—was hovering above Jerusalem ready to destroy it as well.

GABRIEL: He watched David as he repented and stayed His hand from further devastation.

MICHAEL: The Almighty called upon us to judge Israel for David's sin.

GABRIEL: David learned a hard lesson from this choice and turned quickly to closely follow Yahweh and His ways. (24:25)

MICHAEL: We were sent many times to accompany him in his battles with the surrounding nations. Clearly, David was favored in every way as Yahweh's anointed.

GABRIEL: Then Solomon, the appointed heir to follow him to the throne, succeeded even more so, bringing peace and wealth to Israel as never before.

MICHAEL: Also, he was chosen to build the elaborate temple for the worship of King Yahweh in Jerusalem. (1 Kings 6)

GABRIEL: Sadly, after Solomon's bountiful reign, the kingdom divided in two and soon afterward began to fall into ill repute. (1 Kings 12:20)

MICHAEL: Our Master had repeatedly warned them of the misfortune which would follow if they strayed from keeping his commandments, especially worshipping other gods.

GABRIEL: This misfortune was delayed by some kings who brought reform in Judah, the southern kingdom. But eventually, the northern tribes and then the southern tribes were conquered and taken into captivity. (2 Kings 17:6, 25:21)

MICHAEL: Even though his people were unfaithful, Yahweh remained ever true and protected them even in their exile.

GABRIEL: Remember how Esther became a conduit to rescue Israel from certain extermination at the hands of their hosts, the Assyrians and the Babylonians, who were certainly involved in this evil plot?

MICHAEL: Yes, and there are many other examples of God intervening by sending us, His messengers.

GABRIEL: One of the most memorable pertained to one of Yahweh's favored prophets in the land of Babylon—Daniel.

⁂

"So David said to Joab and to the princes of the people, 'Go, count Israel from Beersheba even to Dan, and bring me word that I may know their total count.' . . . And this thing was displeasing in the sight of God, so He struck Israel. . . . So Yahweh sent a pestilence against Israel; and 70,000 men of Israel fell. And God sent an angel to Jerusalem to destroy it; but as he was about to destroy it, Yahweh saw and relented concerning the calamity, and said to the destroying angel, 'It is enough! Now relax your hand.'. . . Then Yahweh spoke to the angel, and he returned his sword to its sheath." (1 Chronicles 21:2, 7, 14–15)

CHAPTER 10

THE ENVISIONING DANIEL

"Then the king arose at dawn, at the break of day, and hurriedly went to the lions' den. When he had come near the den to Daniel, he cried out with a troubled voice. The king answered and said to Daniel, 'Daniel, servant of the living God, has your God, whom you constantly serve, been able to save you from the lions?' Then Daniel spoke to the king, 'O king, live forever! My God sent His angel and shut the lions' mouths, and they have not harmed me, inasmuch as I was found innocent before Him; and also toward you, O king, I have done no harm.' " (Daniel 6:19–22)

■

Yodh

GABRIEL: To invoke all the vital details about Daniel, let us consult with our comrade Mariuk. Please call to mind each of these events for us.

MARIUK: It is my pleasure to be of service in this way. Daniel and his three compatriots were chosen to serve as trained advisors to King Nebuchadnezzar. They showed their highest qualities by refusing the luxurious table of the king. (Daniel 1:8)

MICHAEL: So, what was the result of their choice?

MARIUK: These four proved to be the healthiest and admirable of the young men to be developed for the king's service. Thus, they were allowed to keep their diet pure from the ways of the Babylonian royalty. (1:15–16)

GABRIEL: And did this make a difference for these youths?

MARIUK: When Nebuchadnezzar had a troubling dream which he did not understand, he requested all his magicians, enchanters, sorcerers, and all his wise men tell him his dream and what it meant. (Daniel 2:2–3)

MICHAEL: Were they able to tell the dream to the king?

MARIUK: No, they claimed no one could tell him the dream and asked that he share it. He would not accept this limitation and threaten their extermination if they could not tell him. (2:11)

GABRIEL: When did Daniel become a participant in this situation?

MARIUK: When the king's captain, Arioch, announced the edict of the king to have all the wise men to be killed, Daniel responded intelligently and set up a time to meet with the king to tell him his dream and its interpretation. (2:14–16)

MICHAEL: Did he undertake this challenge on his own?

MARIUK: No, he immediately shared the matter with his fellows. Daniel told them to seek mercy from heaven concerning this mystery that Yahweh would reveal this and save their lives. (2:17–19)

GABRIEL: How did Yahweh answer this humble request?

MARIUK: God resolved the mystery by giving Daniel a vision in the night. And Daniel exalted the God of heaven, acknowledging His wisdom and might. His gratitude was immense in response. (2:20–23)

MICHAEL: What did Daniel do next?

MARIUK: He declared to the captain not to destroy the wise men of Babylon. That he would reveal the mystery to the king. So, the captain gave him audience with the king. (2:24)

GABRIEL: How did Daniel approach the king?

MARIUK: When the king asked him if he could make known his dream and its interpretation, Daniel claimed no one but the true God in heaven could reveal these mysteries. He went on to explain that Yahweh has made known what will be in the latter days. (2:28)

MICHAEL: Whom did he give all the credit?

MARIUK: He took no praise for this revelation but totally proclaimed Yahweh's glory be upheld. Then he described the future kingdoms of the world compared with the various metals and where Babylon fit in this image. (2:31–35)

GABRIEL: How did the king respond to this disclosure?

MARIUK: Nebuchadnezzar was relieved and humbled at this revelation and quickly sought to elevate Daniel and his companions to the highest place of honor. (2:46–49)

MICHAEL: Then peace must have then followed, right?

MARIUK: Actually, King Nebuchadnezzar proceeded to have a golden statue made in his image and all were required to worship him. Shadrach, Meshach and Abednego, however, did not, so they were cast into a fiery furnace. (Daniel 3:1–18)

GABRIEL: How did King Yahweh intervene on their behalf?

MARIUK: The King of creation did not allow even their hair or clothes to be singed by the flames! And then the king of Babylon was forced to acknowledge what Yahweh was able to do. (3:27–28)

MICHAEL: How did he then respond to the Jews?

MARIUK: He saw my presence among them and that Yahweh protected them from the fire in the furnace. And Nebuchadnezzar then decreed that no one would be allowed to even speak against their God. Then he promoted them in the government of Babylon. (3:29–30)

GABRIEL: Was this then the end of the story of Daniel?

MARIUK: No. The king had another dream, and again no one could interpret it. So Daniel was brought in to make it known. (Daniel 4:8)

MICHAEL: What did this reveal to the king?

MARIUK: Daniel told the king that his kingdom would be reduced in power and that Nebuchadnezzar himself would be humbled and live like a beast of the field. (4:19–27)

GABRIEL: How long was the king to live in this state of existence?

MARIUK: Until he realized and honored the Most High as the ruler over all. Furthermore, he was told to break off his sins by practicing righteousness.

MICHAEL: Was Nebuchadnezzar able to carry out this command?

MARIUK: Temporarily he did, but at the end of a year he was walking on the roof of the royal palace and began to admire his works, ultimately acclaiming his own might and glory. (4:29–30)

GABRIEL: Did this bring a response from the Almighty?

MARIUK: Yes, immediately Yahweh spoke from heaven and made it clear that Nebuchadnezzar's kingdom had been taken from him. And the vision of his humiliation would now come to fulfillment. He was transformed to a lowly beast and looked like one as well. (4:31–33)

MICHAEL: Were these the events which changed his direction?

MARIUK: After a period of time. Nebuchadnezzar's reasoning returned to him, and he extolled and honored the King of creation. Thus, his majesty and splendor were returned to him as he gave honor where it was due. (4:34–37)

GABRIEL: Describe the brief interaction Daniel had with the newly crowned Belshazzar, Nebuchadnezzar's son.

MARIUK: Belshazzar was holding a great feast and called for the vessels taken from the temple in Jerusalem to be brought in and used for their wine. Immediately there appeared fingers of a hand writing on the palace wall. It terrified the king, so he called for the wise men to interpret the writing, promising great reward. When no one could read the words, the Queen Mother recommended that Daniel be sought out. (Daniel 5:1–12)

MICHAEL: There is no doubt that King Yahweh would use Daniel to reveal the mystery to Belshazzar.

MARIUK: Unquestionably! As instructed, Daniel clearly delineated the words of the inscription and the meaning of each phrase. God was going to judge the king and that the days of the kingdom were numbered. The words said that the king had been weighed and found

wanting, and the kingdom would be divided between the Medes and the Persians. This all took place even that night as the king was killed, and Darius the Mede received the kingship. (5:25–30)

GABRIEL: And so, Daniel was elevated once again, right?

MARIUK: So much so that all the other officers resented him and sought a plan whereby Daniel would incriminate himself. They knew of his devotion to his God, so they used that against him. They plotted by cunningly convincing the king to sign a law saying that people could petition only him. The penalty for praying to any other god would result in being cast into the lion's den and destroyed. (Daniel 6:6–7)

MICHAEL: Did this edict affect the actions of Daniel?

MARIUK: No. Daniel continued to face Jerusalem three times a day and pray to the Most High. When he was discovered disobeying, these officials confronted him with the words of the king's own injunction. Though this situation distressed the king, he had no choice but to follow through with his word. (6:10–14)

GABRIEL: How then, did it go with Daniel regarding the lions?

MARIUK: Daniel was cast into the lions' den, but first Darius declared to Daniel his earnest desire for his favored servant: "Your God, whom

you constantly serve will Himself save you!" Then the entrance was enclosed, and the king went to his palace and spent the night fasting on behalf of Daniel. (6:16–18)

MICHAEL: That is rather surprising that the king had so much concern for Daniel. What happened next?

MARIUK: Darius arose early and went to check on Daniel, crying out, "Daniel, servant of the living God, has your God, whom you constantly serve, been able to save you from the lions?" And then Daniel informed the king that Yahweh had sent me. And I had shut the lions' mouths. Consequently, they did not harm him. With this report Darius was exceedingly glad and had Daniel taken up from the den. Then the king had those who had maliciously accused Daniel thrown to the lions. (6:19–24)

GABRIEL: Describe how you felt protecting Daniel from the mouths of the lions.

MARIUK: Greatly honored! I felt so privileged that King Yahweh would use me to accomplish such an important task for His people. Of course, this action did not require much of my power since the Majestic One has empowered us immensely to perform His service. I still felt such a sense of satisfaction to be used for His purposes.

MICHAEL: We understand, Mariuk, as we have experienced the same pleasures ourselves many times. What difference did this event have on the king and his kingdom?

MARIUK: The effect was profound for both, as Darius made a decree that all under his dominion are to tremble and fear before the God of Daniel, reflecting his understanding of Yahweh's ability to save. Yahweh thus received much glory with all the people because of this resounding incident. (6:26)

GABRIEL: How wonderful it is to see our Almighty be recognized and honored for who He is. Let us ask Sariel to tell us about the encounter he had with Daniel.

Sariel: Yes, I'm privileged to relay what took place with Daniel regarding his night visions. He foresaw a description of the last days of earth which troubled him deeply, and he asked me for an interpretation of these events. When I showed him, it helped to settle him down from these terrifying revelations. Therefore, he was then able to just keep these matters within his heart as well as relating these visions in his book. (Daniel 7:28)

MICHAEL: And again, a couple of years later, Daniel had another dream. And Gabriel, you were directly involved that time, right?

GABRIEL: Yes, I was called upon to help Daniel then as he had many questions regarding these disturbing images. Tamil, who was observing, asked me for the time parameters that these visions would take place, which I provided. Then Daniel continued to seek understanding of all these descriptions, and that is when the pre-incarnate Christ asked me to respond directly.

MICHAEL: What did you convey to him at that time?

GABRIEL: First, I told him the dreams were concerning the latter days of the earth—the appointed time of the end. I explained what each of the images portrayed and later asked him to seal up the vision since it was regarding the distant future. (Daniel 9:3)

MICHAEL: Did this information help Daniel?

GABRIEL: Not completely, because he then only sought more fervently with prayer and fasting, with sackcloth and ashes to know more. He was earnest in all this due to the calamities which were to come upon God's people, Israel. He pleaded for mercy from this impending judgment. (9:16)

MICHAEL: Is this where you were asked to intervene with Daniel?

GABRIEL: Exactly, I was sent in swift flight to his assistance. I explained that at the beginning of his pleas, I was sent out to tell the meaning. I also conveyed the reason he was getting this response is that he is clearly loved by Yahweh the Great. So, these new pieces of knowledge helped Daniel understand more of the timetable of the tribulation, but he was still troubled deeply. (9:22–27)

MICHAEL: When did Daniel receive more truth about these matters?

GABRIEL: A few years later, when Cyrus ruled Persia, Daniel was given a word in a vision. Daniel had some understanding of the revelation and yet he mourned and fasted for three weeks. Then he was shown a "man" with dazzling appearance before whom all his strength was drained from him, and he fell into a trance. (Daniel 10:1–9)

MICHAEL: Explain how you restored him.

GABRIEL: I touched him and told him, "O Daniel, man of high esteem, understand the words that I am about to speak to you." And here I stood him upright, and as Daniel was trembling, I told him to not be afraid "for from the first day that you gave your heart to understand

this and to humble yourself before your God, your words have been heard, and I have come in response to your words." (10:11–12)

MICHAEL: Is that when you told him that I had come to help you battle the demon prince of Persia?

GABRIEL: Definitely! I made him aware that the prince of Persia had withstood me for twenty-one days as I was coming to him to make him understand what is to happen to Israel in the final years. (10:13)

MICHAEL: How did Daniel respond to these disclosures?

GABRIEL: Once again he was devastated and fell with his face to the ground. Then Jesus (the angel of Yahweh) Himself touched him, and he replied that he had no strength. And so, Jesus touched Daniel again and gave him strength to hear His words: "O man of high esteem, do not be afraid. Peace be with you; gather strength and be strong!" And when he was encouraged, I informed him that I would now return to fight against the demonic prince of Persia and then the prince of Greece. I let him know that you, their prince, would contend along with me on their behalf. (10::18–20)

MICHAEL: How, then, did it end with Daniel?

GABRIEL: He was given other truth about the final days and then told that you, Michael, as the great prince in charge of the nation of Israel, would arise. And even though there would be trouble on earth as never seen before, you would deliver their people (10:21). Finally, Daniel was told to shut up the words and seal the book until the time of the end. In that day many people "will go to and fro, and knowledge will increase." (Daniel 12:4)

MICHAEL: Thus, we had many special encounters with Daniel, the man favored by God. And he was instrumental in communicating many truths, not only for the present time, but for the future.

GABRIEL: Great praises to the Holy One of Israel for allowing us as angels to be helpful in these situations where people need to understand better the King's plan.

MICHAEL: Of course, Yahweh is the One who gets all the credit for these great things that took place!

"Then Nebuchadnezzar the king was astounded and hurriedly stood up; he answered and said to his high officials, "Was it not three men we cast tied up into the midst of the fire?" They answered and said to the king, "Certainly, O king." He answered and said, "Look! I see four men loosed and walking about in the midst of the fire without harm, and the appearance of the fourth is like a son of the gods!" Then Nebuchadnezzar came near to the door of the furnace of blazing fire; he answered and said, "Shadrach, Meshach, and Abed-nego, come out, you servants of the Most High God, and come here!" Then Shadrach, Meshach, and Abed-nego came out of the midst of the fire. Then the satraps, the prefects, the governors, and the king's high officials gathered around and saw in regard to these men that the fire had no power over the bodies of these men, nor was the hair of their head singed, nor were their trousers damaged, nor had the smell of fire even come upon them.

Nebuchadnezzar answered and said, "Blessed be the God of Shadrach, Meshach, and Abed-nego, who has sent His angel and saved His servants who put their trust in Him, violating the king's word, and gave up their bodies so as not to serve and not to worship any god except their own God." (Daniel 3:24–28)

NEW TESTAMENT

THE ASTOUNDING BIRTH

"In the same region there were some shepherds staying out in the fields and keeping watch over their flock by night. And an angel of the Lord stood before them, and the glory of the Lord shone around them; and they were terribly frightened. But the angel said to them, "Do not be afraid; for behold, I bring you good news of great joy which will be for all the people. For today in the city of David there has been born for you a Savior, who is Christ the Lord. And this will be the sign for you: you will find a baby wrapped in cloths and lying in a manger." And suddenly there appeared with the angel a multitude of the heavenly host praising God and saying,

'Glory to God in the highest, and on earth peace among men with whom He is pleased.'

"And it happened that when the angels had gone away from them into heaven, the shepherds began saying to one another, "Let us go to Bethlehem then, and see this thing that has happened which the Lord has made known to us." So they went in a hurry and found their way to Mary and Joseph, and the baby lying in the manger. And when they

had seen this, they made known the statement which had been told them about this Child. And all who heard it marveled at the things which were told them by the shepherds. But Mary was treasuring all these things, pondering them in her heart. And the shepherds went back, glorifying and praising God for all that they had heard and seen, just as was told them." (Luke 2:8–20)

 כ

Kaph

GABRIEL: Now let us look ahead to a time when many prophecies were fulfilled.

MICHAEL: There were four hundred years of silence following Daniel and the prophets.

GABRIEL: Then came the time when numbers of foretellings came to fruition through our wonderful Master!

MICHAEL: How shall we begin to tell this story? I know, let us start with the forecast of the forerunner. You were the chosen messenger, right?

GABRIEL: The Almighty sent me with an amazing announcement to give to the priest Zachariah, whose wife, Elizabeth, had been barren for many long years.

MICHAEL: Explain how you approached him with your message.

GABRIEL: As a priest, Zachariah was chosen by lot to represent his division to enter the Holy of Holies to burn incense before Yahweh. (Luke 1:8–9)

MICHAEL: It was a very important task he was given the honor of performing. How then did it go when you met him?

GABRIEL: I appeared to him beside the altar of incense. And, of course, he was troubled at seeing me. Fear overcame him. (1:11–12)

MICHAEL: Humans are always in awe of us because of our great height (fifteen feet), wingspan (thirty feet) and radiant, golden glow.

GABRIEL: Hence our first words are always, "Fear not!" when we are coming with good news.

MICHAEL: You were there to announce an end to his wife's barrenness, which was exceptionally positive news.

GABRIEL: I relayed that their prayers had been answered by way of a son that was to be born to Elizabeth, and whose name would be called John. I even affirmed the joy and gladness to be experienced by many. (1:13–14)

MICHAEL: That was also due to John's greatness before the Lord, and thus he was to be separated from strong drink, to be filled with the Holy Spirit even prior to his birth.

GABRIEL: Yes, his ministry would turn many from disobedience to Yahweh. This would prepare the way for the coming Messiah.

MICHAEL: Describe Zachariah's response to your announcement.

GABRIEL: He disbelieved and questioned the validity of my news. (1:18)

MICHAEL: What was your next step with him?

GABRIEL: I answered him by stating my name and the fact that I stand in the presence of God Himself. I confirmed that I was sent to tell this good news to him, and that because of his unbelief, he was struck mute until the prediction was fulfilled. (1:19–20)

MICHAEL: How did people react when he came out of the temple?

GABRIEL: They had noticed the delay and wondered at his inability to speak. Many concluded that Zachariah had seen a vision in the temple and questioned what message was communicated. (1:21–22)

MICHAEL: And in due time, Elizabeth did conceive, as foretold, and then she recognized the significance of what Yahweh had done for her.

GABRIEL: She recognized that her reproach had been taken away and that God was doing something special here. (1:24–25)

MICHAEL: I know this was not the last visit you made to Israel.

GABRIEL: No, King Yahweh also sent me on another mission. This time it was to a city in Galilee named Nazareth, to a virgin called Mary, who

was engaged to be married to a man named Joseph, who was of the house of David.

Michael: Describe this conversation with Mary.

Gabriel: I greeted her as a favored one, telling her that Yahweh was with her. However, she was troubled by the encounter, and she was trying to make sense of all this. (1:28)

Michael: Was there some fear mingled in for her as well?

Gabriel: Absolutely, I sought to calm her and emphasized she was being given a great honor by God. I went on to explain that she was to conceive and bear a son who would be called Jesus. (1:30–31)

Michael: Did you explain the meaning of this to Mary?

Gabriel: Definitely! I told her He would be great and would be called the Son of the Most High. Furthermore, I relayed that the Lord God would give Him the throne of his father David and that He would reign over the House of Jacob forever, and His kingdom will never end. (1:32–33)

Michael: What was Mary's response to all this?

GABRIEL: Her question was a good one: "How will this be, since I am a virgin?" she asked. (1:34)

MICHAEL: How did you handle this entreaty?

GABRIEL: I explained as clearly as I could that the process would involve the Holy Spirit's coming upon her, and so the power of the Most High would overshadow her. He would bring this about in a way that the child to be born would be called holy, the Son of God! (1:35)

MICHAEL: You then linked your first appearance to this one, right?

GABRIEL: It was important for Mary to know that her cousin Elizabeth had also conceived even in her old age. Nothing is impossible with God! (1:36)

MICHAEL: And how did Mary receive this revelation?

GABRIEL: Most humbly she submitted herself to the King's plan as His servant and willingly accepted all that Yahweh had designed for her. Witnessing her receptivity and with gladness in my heart, I departed her company. (1:38)

MICHAEL: Meanwhile, another scenario was developing with her fiancé, Joseph, right?

GABRIEL: Without a doubt. Joseph had some pointed questions about her pregnancy. Since they had remained pure, he knew perfectly well that this child was not his.

MICHAEL: What then was Joseph's plan?

GABRIEL: He knew he couldn't in good conscience marry her, but, at the same time, didn't want to publicly humiliate her. Therefore, he decided to just divorce her quietly and not make a big scene. (Matthew 1:19)

MICHAEL: But Joseph's dream changed all that, did it not?

GABRIEL: Correct. Yahweh had me appeared to him as he slept, settling his fears of marrying her. I clearly stated that the child conceived in Mary was, in fact, a result of the Holy Spirit and therefore most holy. (1:20)

MICHAEL: You went on to impart the significance of the child, right?

GABRIEL: Yes, I impressed upon Joseph that this child would be a son, and was to be called Jesus since this means Yahweh saves, which Jesus would do. (1:21)

MICHAEL: Of course, this dream greatly affected Joseph's plans.

GABRIEL: When Joseph awoke, he carried out what had been commanded and took Mary as his wife, but not consummating their marriage until after she had given birth to Jesus. (1:24–25)

MICHAEL: And, speaking of that, let us discuss one of the most significant events for the benefit of all mankind.

GABRIEL: You were involved in this encounter, were you not?

MICHAEL: We all were, but I was privileged to make the announcement to the shepherds in the field that night with the glory of Yahweh shining all around them. (Luke 2:8–9)

GABRIEL: How would you describe the shepherd's reaction?

MICHAEL: Understandably, they demonstrated fear, and I sought to put them at ease, telling them I was bringing them good news of a great joy for all the people. (2:10)

GABRIEL: What were your next words of explanation?

MICHAEL: I told them that this day in the city of David, Bethlehem, a Savior who is Messiah, the Lord, was born. I told them to look for a baby wrapped in swaddling clothes and lying in a manger. (2:11–12)

GABRIEL: That was when all the rest of us converged on the scene, right?

MICHAEL: Yes, the situation was of such magnitude that many of us were called upon to praise the Almighty and declare His glory. We proclaimed the resulting peace on earth among those with whom Yahweh is pleased. (2:13–14)

GABRIEL: So, our King was thus honored, and the shepherds were directed to where they would find the newborn Jesus.

MICHAEL: After having celebrated the miraculous birth, we all return to our positions back in heaven.

GABRIEL: But there was another interaction with Joseph around this time.

MICHAEL: When Herod, the king of Israel, heard the news of the birth of the King of the Jews from the wise men of the east, he was curious, then in turn became extremely troubled. (Matthew 2:3)

GABRIEL: He figured out from them the time when the star appeared. Eventually, when he saw that the wise men were not returning to give an update to Herod, he grew furious. (2:7, 16)

MICHAEL: This became a danger for Joseph, Mary, and Jesus. Thus, you warned him in a dream.

GABRIEL: I told him to take the child and his mother to Egypt for a time until it was safe to return. (2:13)

MICHAEL: In light of Herod's desire to destroy the Child, this was a crafty plan, for the danger was imminent.

GABRIEL: Herod sent his troops to kill all the male children at Bethlehem, two years old and younger. (2:16)

MICHAEL: In this way the child was protected from the slaughter. And later in another dream, you made Joseph aware that it was now safe to return after Herod had died. (2:19–20)

GABRIEL: Joseph heeded my instruction and went back to the land of Israel. Instead of going back to Judea, because Herod's son was now reigning over Judea, Joseph withdrew to the district of Galilee—to Nazareth—to fulfill yet another prophecy. (2:22–23)

"Now the birth of Jesus Christ was as follows: when His mother Mary had been betrothed to Joseph, before they came together she was found to be with child by the Holy Spirit. And Joseph her husband, being a righteous man and not wanting to disgrace her, planned to send her away secretly. But when he had considered this, behold, an angel of the Lord appeared to him in a dream, saying, 'Joseph, son of David, do not be afraid to take Mary as your wife; for the One who has been conceived in her is of the Holy Spirit. And she will bear a Son; and you shall call His name Jesus, for He will save His people from their sins.' Now all this took place in order that what was spoken by the Lord through the prophet would be fulfilled, saying, 'Behold, the virgin shall be with child and shall bear a Son, and they shall call His name Immanuel,' which translated means, 'God with us.' And Joseph got up from his sleep and did as the angel of the Lord commanded him, and took Mary as his wife, but kept her a virgin until she gave birth to a Son; and he called His name Jesus."
(Matthew 1:18–25)

THE LEGITIMIZING TEMPTATION

"And after He had fasted forty days and forty nights, He then became hungry. And the tempter came and said to Him, 'If You are the Son of God, command that these stones become bread.' But He answered and said, 'It is written, "Man shall not live on bread alone, but on every word that proceeds out of the mouth of God." '

"Then the devil took Him into the holy city and had Him stand on the pinnacle of the temple, and said to Him, 'If You are the Son of God, throw Yourself down; for it is written,

"He will command His angels concerning You";

and

"On their hands they will bear You up,

Lest You strike Your foot against a stone." '

"Jesus said to him, 'Again, it is written, "You shall not put the Lord your God to the test." '

"Again, the devil took Him to a very high mountain and showed Him all the kingdoms of the world and their glory; and he said to Him, 'All these things I will give You, if You fall down and worship

me.' Then Jesus said to him, 'Go, Satan! For it is written, "You shall worship the Lord your God, and serve Him only." ' Then the devil left Him; and behold, angels came and began to minister to Him." (Matthew 2:2–11)

Lamedh

GABRIEL: The next time we were involved was at the beginning of Jesus' ministry, when He was about thirty years of age.

MICHAEL: He had just been baptized by John, at which time the Holy Spirit fell on Him like a dove and the Father voiced His pleasure in His beloved Son. (Matthew 3:16–17)

GABRIEL: In preparation for His ministry, Jesus was led by the Spirit into the wilderness to be tested by the devil. (Matthew 4:1)

MICHAEL: And this is about temptation, which the word of Yahweh has much to say.

GABRIEL: The apostle James tells men that when they are tempted not to say " 'I am being tempted by God,' For God cannot be tempted with evil, and He Himself does not tempt anyone." (James 1:13)

MICHAEL: We know that Yahweh does not have the capacity for evil in His essence for He is holy—that means separated from all impurity.

GABRIEL: His perfection also includes goodness, which precludes anything bad or having ill will. He only wants what brings positive results for His creation.

MICHAEL: Consequently, Jesus' temptation had to do with His humanness, which, in fact, could be affected.

GABRIEL: Truly His human nature was susceptible to sin, whereas His godhood could not be persuaded.

MICHAEL: Therefore, Jesus' temptation was real, not imaginary, as Hebrews 4:15 says, "For we do not have a high priest who cannot sympathize with our weaknesses, but One who has been tempted in all things like we are, yet without sin."

GABRIEL: There are three types of temptation John the apostle refers to: "the lust of the flesh and the lust of the eyes and the boastful pride of life" (1 John 2:16).

MICHAEL: We see these three temptations—which are the enemies of God and therefore our enemies— played out in Jesus' temptations. Concerning the world, Jesus was tempted to cast Himself off the pinnacle of the temple. (Matthew 4:5)

GABRIEL: Relating to the flesh, Jesus was tempted to turn the stones into bread because after fasting for forty days He was hungry. (4:3)

MICHAEL: Finally, regarding the devil, He was tempted by Satan to worship him to have dominion over all the world that Satan reigns over. (4:9)

GABRIEL: After Jesus had fasted for forty days and nights and became hungry, the tempter incited Him to turn stones into bread.

MICHAEL: Jesus' response was amazing: "Man shall not live by bread alone, but on every word that proceeds out of the mouth of God" (4:4).

GABRIEL: Like Job of old we see Satan having been given the power to afflict Jesus because Yahweh allowed it.

MICHAEL: He had wanted to prove to Satan that Job was a true example of a righteous man.

GABRIEL: Clearly Yahweh had given Job his faith, which, like Abraham, was counted to him as righteousness.

MICHAEL: Satan, the fallen leader of the rebellion of angels, also called Lucifer, has only malicious intent—to lie, steal, and destroy.

GABRIEL: The devil has devised to thwart every plan of Yahweh through every means possible.

MICHAEL: Thus, it has been from the beginning of creation. Satan has continually sought to destroy God's plan of redemption.

GABRIEL: We saw this in the Garden of Eden when he got Eve questioning the truth and goodness of Yahweh. (Genesis 3:4)

MICHAEL: Even Moses was prompted to strike the rock to get water even though he was told only to speak to it. (Numbers 20:10)

GABRIEL: King David, a man after God's own heart, succumbed to the temptation of Bathsheba and then tried to cover it up by having her husband, Uriah, killed. (2 Samuel 11:26)

MICHAEL: Elijah the Prophet began to believe the lie that only he had not bent the knee to false gods. (1 Kings 19:10)

GABRIEL: Therefore, the devil sought the downfall of Jesus first by tempting Him to turn the stones to bread (Matthew 4:3). Then He was taken to the pinnacle of the temple and challenged to throw Himself down, claiming the Father would send angels to protect Him. (4:5)

MICHAEL: Jesus immediately dispensed this thought by declaring "You shall not put the Lord your God to the test." (Matthew 4:7)

GABRIEL: Consequently, the devil was told this testing of Jesus was not right—a firm rebuke to the evil one!

MICHAEL: Lastly, Satan took Jesus to a very high mountain and showed Him all the kingdoms of the world and their glory. (4:8)

GABRIEL: He promised that if Jesus would only bow down to worship him, he would give all these kingdoms to Him.

MICHAEL: This offer involved quite a deception because, yes, Satan had been given the rule over the kingdoms and dominions on earth, but only temporarily.

GABRIEL: That power was only given to the evil one for a time and ultimately Yahweh reigns overall.

MICHAEL: Yahweh's total sovereignty will be seen completely before the end.

GABRIEL: Yes, Satan only thinks he is all-powerful.

MICHAEL: Consequently, Jesus dismissed Satan and told him to leave Him alone, reminding him that worship is only due to Yahweh. (4:10)

GABRIEL: It is our Master who alone is to be served, not him.

MICHAEL: And this continues to be the message that we pure angels proclaim: worship Yahweh alone and have no other gods before you!

GABRIEL: Our wonderful Master must be worshipped for who He is!

MICHAEL: After Jesus was confronted with these three trials, having fully resisted and rebuked Satan, he left Him alone.

GABRIEL: That is when we were sent to minister to Jesus both physically and emotionally, for these temptations on Him had been severe. (4:11)

MICHAEL: It was apparent that Jesus needed assistance because not only was He fully God, but He was also fully man.

GABRIEL: Thus, He had real needs, just like all humans.

MICHAEL: It was so meaningful to serve Him in these ways, since normally He is the one helping us.

GABRIEL: Seeing Him in a needy condition was unusual to say the least and rewarding at the same time for us ministers of the Most High.

MICHAEL: Our next recorded appearance came as the days of the Lord Jesus on earth were coming to a close.

ᴄ℮

"Now it happened that in those days Jesus came from Nazareth in Galilee and was baptized by John in the Jordan. And immediately coming up out of the water, He saw the heavens opening, and the Spirit like a dove descending upon Him; and a voice came out of the heavens: 'You are My beloved Son, in You I am well-pleased.'

And immediately the Spirit drove Him to go out into the wilderness. And He was in the wilderness forty days being tempted by Satan; and He was with the wild beasts, and the angels were ministering to Him." (Mark 1:9–13)

CHAPTER 13

THE AGONIZING GARDEN

"And He came out and went as was His custom to the Mount of Olives; and the disciples also followed Him. Now when He arrived at the place, He said to them, 'Pray that you may not enter into temptation.' And He withdrew from them about a stone's throw, and He knelt down and began to pray, saying, 'Father, if You are willing, remove this cup from Me, yet not My will, but Yours be done.' Now an angel from heaven appeared to Him, strengthening Him. And being in agony He was praying very fervently, and His sweat became like drops of blood, falling down upon the ground. And when He rose from prayer, He came to the disciples and found them sleeping from sorrow, and said to them, 'Why are you sleeping? Rise up and pray that you may not enter into temptation.' " Luke 22:39–46)

Mem

GABRIEL: As King Jesus faced the prospect of bearing the weight of the sin of the world, He prayed and pleaded that if there was another way to accomplish the Father's will, that the cup of the Father's wrath would be removed from Him.

MICHAEL: Jesus knew completely what this bitter path would mean for Him experientially, and so He grieved, even to the point of sweating blood. (Luke 22:44)

GABRIEL: He obviously needed support in taking those last steps, which was when we came onto the scene. Somewhat like the strengthening we gave Him after the temptations, except that act cost Him His very life.

MICHAEL: Physical torment, as excruciating as it was, did not compare with the spiritual and emotional trauma He endured!

GABRIEL: This agony was clearly predicted by the psalmists in a number of places. I particularly recall Psalm 142:

> "With my voice to Yahweh, I cry aloud;
> With my voice to Yahweh, I make supplication.
> I pour out my complaint before Him;
> I declare my distress before Him.
> When my spirit was faint within me,

You knew my path.

In the way where I walk

They have hidden a trap for me.

Look to the right and see;

That there is no one who regards me;

A way of escape has been destroyed from me;

No one cares for my soul.

I cried out to You, O Yahweh;

I said, 'You are my refuge,

My portion in the land of the living.

Give heed to my cry of lamentation,

For I am brought very low;

Deliver me from my persecutors,

For they are too strong for me.

Bring my soul out of prison,

To give thanks to Your name;

The righteous will encircle me,

For You will deal bountifully with me.' "

MICHAEL: Also, Psalm 62 certainly was another He quoted:

"Surely my soul waits in silence for God;

From Him is my salvation.

Surely He is my rock and my salvation,

My stronghold; I shall not be greatly shaken." (vv. 1–2)

GABRIEL: Psalm 63 continues this expression of pain:

> "O God, You are my God; I shall seek You earnestly;
> My soul thirsts for You, my flesh yearns for You,
> In a dry and weary land without water." (v. 1)

MICHAEL: Parts of Psalm 32 also express His mournful plea:

> "When I kept silent about my sin, my bones wasted away
> Through my groaning all day long.
> For day and night Your hand was heavy upon me;
> My vitality was drained away as with the heat of summer." (vv. 3–4)

GABRIEL: Through it all, Jesus placed his confidence in His Father, as seen in Psalm 18:

> "He said, "I love You, O Yahweh, my strength."
> Yahweh is my rock and my fortress and my deliverer,
> My God, my rock, in whom I take refuge;
> My shield and the horn of my salvation, my stronghold." (vv. 1–2)

MICHAEL: There are numerous other examples of His trust in Yahweh. Some of them were fulfilled precisely in the New Testament, such as when the psalmist wrote:

> "My God, my God, why have You forsaken me?
> Far from my salvation are the words of my groaning.

O my God, I call by day, but You do not answer;

And by night, but I have no rest." (Psalm 22:1–2)

GABRIEL: In the same Psalm Jesus' experience is depicted as follows:

"I am poured out like water,

And all my bones are out of joint;

My heart is like wax;

It is melted within me.

My strength is dried up like a potsherd,

And my tongue cleaves to my jaws;

And You lay me in the dust of death.

For dogs have surrounded me;

A band of evildoers has encompassed me;

They pierced my hands and my feet.

I count all my bones.

They look, they stare at me;

They divide my garments among them,

And for my clothing they cast lots." (Psalm 22:14–18)

MICHAEL: Another vivid fulfillment can be seen in Psalm 31 where Jesus relinquishes His life as a man:

> "Into Your hand I commit my spirit;
> You have ransomed me, O Yahweh, God of truth." (v. 5)

GABRIEL: Hence the stark realities had long been predicted about Jesus' suffering and death.

MICHAEL: This grief in the garden was consequently not a surprise, and, in fact, knowing in advance what would happen only added to the weight of His burden.

GABRIEL: He was about to experience the massive weight of the sin of the whole world for all time, falling upon His shoulders!

MICHAEL: When the transfer took place, Jesus would be separated from the Father's gaze for the first time ever.

GABRIEL: In fact, the Almighty Father would turn from Him at that time because He cannot associate with sin due to His holiness.

MICHAEL: All this pain was at the forefront of Jesus' mind as He contemplated the road that lay ahead for Him.

GABRIEL: That was why we were called upon to strengthen Him.

MICHAEL: Jesus made an interesting comment in the Garden of Gethsemane during the arrest by the mob sent by the chief priests and elders.

GABRIEL: Yes, when they laid their hands on Jesus to seize Him, one of Jesus' disciples drew his sword and cut off the ear of the servant of the high priest.

MICHAEL: Jesus commanded His disciple to put away his sword and asked, "Do you think that I cannot appeal to My Father, and He will at once put at My disposal more than twelve legions of angels?" (Matthew 26:53)

GABRIEL: With certainty, Jesus knew they were ready to come to His aid at any moment. All we needed was to be given the word by the Father and it would be done.

MICHAEL: What amazes me about Jesus' remark is that he said only twelve legions when in reality, instead of twelve thousand many millions were available at His beckon call.

GABRIEL: I am sure that He got His point across with His question. But His understatement is noteworthy!

"And He took with Him Peter and James and John, and began to be very distressed and troubled. And He aid to them, 'My soul is deeply grieved to the point of death; remain here and keep watch.' And He went a little beyond them, and fell to the ground and began to pray that if it were possible, the hour might pass from Him. And He was saying, 'Abba! Father! All things are possible for You; remove this cup from Me; yet not what I will, but what You will.' And He came and found them sleeping, and said to Peter, 'Simon, are you sleeping? Could you not keep watch for one hour? Keep watching and praying that you may not come into temptation; the spirit is willing, but the flesh is weak.' And again He went away and prayed, saying the same words. And again He came and found them sleeping, for their eyes were very heavy; and they did not know what to answer Him. And He came the third time, and said to them, 'Are you still sleeping and resting? It is enough; the hour has come; behold, the Son of Man is being betrayed into the hands of sinners. Get up, let us go; behold, the one who betrays Me is at hand!' " (Mark 14:33–42)

CHAPTER 14

THE ENLIVENING CLOSURES

"Now after the Sabbath, as it began to dawn toward the first day of the week, Mary Magdalene and the other Mary came to look at the grave. And behold, there was a great earthquake, for an angel of the Lord descended from heaven and came and rolled away the stone and sat upon it. And his appearance was like lightning, and his clothing as white as snow. And the guards quaked from fear of him and became like dead men. And the angel answered and said to the women, 'Do not be afraid; for I know that you are looking for Jesus who has been crucified. He is not here, for He has risen, just as He said. Come, see the place where He was lying. And go quickly and tell His disciples that He has risen from the dead; and behold, He is going ahead of you into Galilee, there you will see Him; behold, I have told you.'

"And they left the tomb quickly with fear and great joy and ran to report it to His disciples. And behold, Jesus met them and said, 'Greetings!' And they came up and took hold of His feet and

worshiped Him. Then Jesus said to them, "Do not be afraid; go and report to My brothers to leave for Galilee, and there they will see Me." (Matthew 28:1–10)

ב

Nun

MICHAEL: The events that followed the betrayal by Judas; arrest by the officers; and trials before the high priest, Pilate, and Herod ended, as we know, with Jesus being brutally scourged, forced to carry His cross, nailed to it, and left on it until dead.

GABRIEL: Joseph of Arimathea quickly took Jesus' body to a nearby tomb before the Sabbath began that evening. (Matthew 27:57–60)

MICHAEL: His disciples and the women who had followed Him witnessed His body being placed in the tomb. (27:61)

GABRIEL: Most of the disciples were hopeless during this period and wondered what they should do.

MICHAEL: Let us turn to the events after the crucifixion and when we appeared at Jesus' tomb.

GABRIEL: You and I, in fact, had a task to complete before anyone arrived. We descended from heaven, causing an earthquake.

MICHAEL: We rolled the stone back from the tomb opening and then sat on it. Our appearance and clothing were dazzling white. (Luke 24:4)

GABRIEL: Upon seeing us, the guards were so fearful they trembled and became like dead men. (Matthew 28:4)

MICHAEL: Consequently, when Mary Magdalene and the other Mary arrived at the tomb that early Sunday morning, they found the large stone rolled away. (Luke 24:2)

GABRIEL: Jesus was no longer to be found inside, and they were perplexed about this. As they entered, they were startled by you and I standing beside them in our dazzling white apparel. (Matthew 28:3; Luke 24:4; Mark 16:5)

MICHAEL: With the puzzled look on their faces, you knew they needed to be comforted.

GABRIEL: I said, "Do not be amazed; you are looking for Jesus the Nazarene, who has been crucified. He has risen; He is not here." (16:6)

MICHAEL: Then I told them to examine the place where He had been laid and reminded them of Jesus' words that the Son of Man must be delivered into the hands of sinful men and be crucified then on the third day rise. (Luke 24:6)

GABRIEL: Accordingly, we encouraged them to go quickly and tell the disciples that He has risen from the dead. (Mark 16:7)

MICHAEL: When the women ran and relayed the message to the others, Peter and John raced to the tomb to see for themselves. (John 20:3–4)

GABRIEL: John reached the tomb first but did not go in, just stooping to look in. Characteristically, Peter barged right in, and he saw the linen clothes lying there. (20:5–6)

MICHAEL: They also noticed the face cloth was not lying with the linen cloths but folded up in a place by itself. (20:7)

GABRIEL: When John did enter, he saw and believed, for until now none of the disciples understood the Scripture, that He must rise from the dead. (20:8)

MICHAEL: It was at this point that we had an additional conversation with the women.

GABRIEL: As they stood weeping outside the tomb and looked in again, we manifested ourselves to them and asked Mary why she was weeping. (20:13)

MICHAEL: She responded, "They have taken away my Lord, and I do not know where they have laid Him." (20:13)

GABRIEL: Thus, we watched as the scene unfolded. She turned and saw Jesus standing near; however, He had cloaked His identity to her. (20:14)

MICHAEL: Jesus spoke to her, saying, "Woman, why are you crying? Whom are you seeking?" (20:15)

GABRIEL: Mistaking Him to be the gardener, she said to Him, "Sir, if you have carried Him away, tell me where you have laid Him, and I will take Him away." (20:16)

MICHAEL: Jesus now spoke her name and simultaneously she recognized Him and exclaimed "Rabboni!" (which means, Teacher), and hugged Him tightly. (20:16)

GABRIEL: He told her not to cling to Him since He had not yet ascended to the Father (20:17). And, in fact, the ascension is our next stop along the way.

MICHAEL: Okay, dear Gabriel, my cohort in service to the great Yahweh, let us look forward to this time when Jesus' tenure on earth was coming to an end.

GABRIEL: My true comrade in ministry, there were some interesting interactions with the human disciples at this time.

MICHAEL: During those forty days after His suffering Jesus presented Himself alive, speaking numbers of truths about the kingdom of God.

GABRIEL: While He was staying with them, He ordered them not to depart from Jerusalem, but to wait for the promise of the Father. (Luke 24:49)

MICHAEL: He was preparing them for their baptism with the Holy Spirit, who was to come soon.

GABRIEL: When they asked Jesus if He would at this time restore the kingdom to Israel, He responded, "It is not for you to know times or seasons that the Father has fixed by His own authority."

MICHAEL: Then He went on to explain that it was not for them to know times and seasons but that they would receive power when the Holy Spirit came upon them. So that they would "Be My witnesses in

Jerusalem, and in all Judea and Samaria, and to the end of the earth." (Acts 1:7–8)

GABRIEL: When He had finished saying these truths, as they were looking on, Jesus was lifted up, and a cloud took Him out of their sight. (1:9)

MICHAEL: And this is where we enter the picture. While they were still gazing into heaven to try to see Jesus, you said to them, "Men of Galilee, why do you stand looking toward heaven? This Jesus, who was taken up from you into heaven, will come in the same way as you saw Him go into heaven." (1:11)

GABRIEL: Then they left the Mount of Olives where this took place and returned to Jerusalem. (1:12)

MICHAEL: They went away treasuring all these things in their hearts. And looked forward to the continuing ministry they would have for Jesus.

GABRIEL: Being involved in this most crucial event in the life of our Lord was thoroughly rewarding.

MICHAEL: It certainly was humbling to be used to interact with humans at that powerful juncture.

GABRIEL: Much praise and glory to the Maker and Master as He carried out His plans made from before time.

MICHAEL: What a magnificent and magnanimous King we serve, and may His name, Yahweh, be lifted up forever!

GABRIEL: Yes, He deserves all the credit for the gracious gift He gave in His son's life, burial, and resurrection.

"So when they had come together, they were asking Him, saying, 'Lord, is it at this time You are restoring the kingdom to Israel?' But He said to them, 'It is not for you to know times or seasons which the Father has set by His own authority; but you will receive power when the Holy Spirit has come upon you; and you shall be My witnesses both in Jerusalem, and in all Judea and Samaria, and even to the end of the earth.'

"And after He had said these things, He was lifted up while they were looking on, and a cloud received Him out of their sight. And as they were gazing intently into the sky while He was going, behold, two men in white clothing stood beside them. They also said, 'Men of Galilee, why do you stand looking toward heaven? This Jesus, who has been taken up from you into heaven, will come in just the same way as you have watched Him go into heaven.' " (Acts 1:6–11)

CHAPTER 15

THE INTERVENING ACTIVITIES

"Now there was a man at Caesarea named Cornelius, a centurion of what was called the Italian cohort, a devout man and one who feared God with all his household, and gave many alms to the people and prayed to God continually. About the ninth hour of the day he clearly saw in a vision an angel of God who had come in and said to him, 'Cornelius!' And looking intently on him and becoming afraid, he said, 'What is it, Lord?' And he said to him, 'Your prayers and alms have ascended as a memorial before God Now send some men to Joppa and summon a man named Simon, who is also called Peter; he is lodging with a tanner named Simon, whose house is by the sea.' And when the angel who was speaking to him had left, he called two of his servants and a devout soldier of those who were his personal attendants, and after he explained everything to them, he sent them to Joppa." (Acts 10:1–8)

Samekh

MICHAEL: There were many additional times we played a part in ministry to humans. For instance, there was the situation with Cornelius.

GABRIEL: Absolutely, let us take some time to reflect on this. Cornelius was a Roman commander who was known as a devout man who feared God. He gave money generously to the people and prayed to the Father continually.

MICHAEL: You appeared to this man in a vision during the day and called him by name. (Acts 10:3)

GABRIEL: Cornelius stared at me in terror and asked, "What is it, Lord?" I replied "Your prayers and alms have ascended as a memorial before God. Now send men to Joppa and summon a man named Simon, who is also called Peter." (10:4–5)

MICHAEL: You then explained to him that Peter was lodging with Simon, a tanner whose house is by the seaside in Joppa.

GABRIEL: Cornelius seemed to understand my direction, and when I left, he proceeded to Simon's house.

MICHAEL: And we know what transpired as a result. As the envoy was approaching the city, Peter was having his own surprising vision.

GABRIEL: He had gone to the tanner's rooftop to pray. He started to get hungry, and while the food was being prepared, he fell into a trance. (10:9–10)

MICHAEL: In his vision, Peter saw the heavens open and something like a great sheet descending, being let down by its four corners upon the earth. (10:11)

GABRIEL: In it were all kinds of animals and reptiles and birds of the air. He was instructed by a voice: "Rise up, Peter, slaughter and eat." (10:13)

MICHAEL: But he objected, noting that he had "never eaten anything defiled and unclean." (10:14)

GABRIEL: The Father spoke again, this time saying, "What God has cleansed, no longer consider defiled." (10:15)

MICHAEL: After this happened three times, the sheet with the various animals was taken up at once to heaven. (10:16)

GABRIEL: Clearly this occurring three times indicated it was from Yahweh Himself.

MICHAEL: The message the Most High gave Peter was that Gentiles were no longer to be unclean; they now were to be recipients of the gospel by grace through faith.

GABRIEL: Yahweh, therefore, was giving Peter permission to fraternize with the Goim, the nations. And he was about to encounter such a situation.

MICHAEL: Immediately the men sent by Cornelius arrived at Simon's gate and asked for Peter.

GABRIEL: The Spirit related to Peter that the men were sent by Yahweh and that he should accompany them without hesitation. (10:19–20)

MICHAEL: This was all part of the Divine plan, and Peter complied.

GABRIEL: When Peter requested the reason for their coming, they related Cornelius's story about how he was directed by an angel to ask Peter to come and present the good news to him and his household. (10:22)

MICHAEL: After confirming God's intervention twice, Peter commenced to recount the events surrounding Jesus' ministry, life, death, and resurrection.

GABRIEL: Even while Peter was finishing his speech, the Holy Spirit fell on all who heard his words. So indeed, even Gentiles were now counted among Jesus' children, and they were physically baptized as well.

MICHAEL: And so Peter related this story to all the apostles and brothers back in Jerusalem and they glorified Yahweh declaring, "Well then, God has granted to the Gentiles also repentance that leads to life." (Acts 11:18)

GABRIEL: What a momentous occasion. So grateful when His Majesty lets us be a part of His plans.

MICHAEL: However, another invention involved a more difficult situation regarding persecution.

GABRIEL: The church leaders were now being killed and arrested, and even Peter was targeted and imprisoned.

MICHAEL: He was bound with two chains and slept between two soldiers while other sentries were at the entrance guarding the prison (Acts 12:6). And that is when Zaphkiel was called upon, so let us get the story directly from him. How did it happen?

ZAPHKIEL: I was sent to Peter in prison and stood next to him, and my light shone in the cell. (12:7)

MICHAEL: Tell us what took place next.

ZAPHKIEL: I struck Peter on the side, waking him, and then I instructed him to "get up quickly! Then I loosened the chains from his hands. (12:7)

GABRIEL: How did you proceed after doing this?

ZAPHKIEL: I told him to dress himself and to put on his sandals, and he did so. I asked him to wrap his cloak around him and to follow me. (12:8)

MICHAEL: And what was Peter's reaction?

ZAPHKIEL: I'm not sure he thought this was really happening and maybe it was only a vision. But when I led him past the first and second guards and to the iron gate leading into the city, I think reality set in—especially when the gate opened on its own, and we went out. We went along one street and then I left him.

GABRIEL: And I heard that Peter recounted that when he "came to himself," he said, "Now truly I know that the Lord has sent His angel

and rescued me from the hand of Herod and from all that the Jewish people were expecting." (12:11)

MICHAEL: Having come to his senses, Peter went to the gathering of the disciples and knocked at the door. (12:13)

GABRIEL: There was disbelief at first, and then amazement and joy at God's rescue, which Peter relayed to them. (12:14–16)

MICHAEL: Paul experienced a similar type of deliverance in Philippi when he was in prison, and we opened all the doors via an earthquake so that he was set free. (Acts 16:26)

GABRIEL: And the result in that case was that the jailer and all his household became Christians through Paul's ministry. (16:33)

MICHAEL: This came about because Paul kept all the prisoners intact since they did not leave the jail.

GABRIEL: Paul also had a great impact during a storm at sea when they all feared they would be killed in the shipwreck.

MICHAEL: He encouraged the shipmates to take heart, and he recounted the assurance he had received from you that very night. (Acts 27:23)

GABRIEL: Indeed, I passed along Yahweh's word, "Do not be afraid, Paul; you must stand before Caesar; and behold, God has granted you all those who are sailing with you." (27:24)

MICHAEL: Thus, they were encouraged to have faith in God like him, "that it will turn out exactly as I have been told. But we must run aground on some island." (27:25–26)

GABRIEL: Absolutely. It did transpire just as God had promised. The Almighty always keeps His promises!

"Now on the very night when Herod was about to bring him forward, Peter was sleeping between two soldiers, bound with two chains, and guards in front of the door were watching over the prison. And behold, an angel of the Lord suddenly appeared and a light shone in the cell; and he struck Peter's side and woke him up, saying, 'Rise up quickly.' And his chains fell off his hands. And the angel said to him, 'Gird yourself and put on your sandals.' And he did so. And he said to him, 'Wrap your garment around yourself and follow me.' And he went out and continued to follow, and he did not know that what was being done by the angel was real, but was thinking he was seeing a vision. And when they had passed the first and second guard posts, they came to the iron gate that leads into the city, which opened for them by itself; and they went out and went along one street, and immediately the angel departed from him. When Peter came to himself, he said, 'Now truly I know that the Lord has sent His angel and rescued me from the hand of Herod and from all that the Jewish people were expecting.' And when he realized this, he went to the house of Mary, the mother of John who was also called Mark, where many were gathered together and were praying. And when he knocked at the door of the gate, a servant-girl named Rhoda came to answer. And when she recognized Peter's voice, because of her joy she did not open the gate. But she ran in and reported that Peter was standing in front of the gate. And they said to her, 'You are out of your mind!' But

she kept insisting that it was so. They kept saying, 'It is his angel.' But Peter continued knocking, and when they opened the door, they saw him and were astounded. But motioning to them with his hand to be silent, he recounted to them how the Lord had led him out of the prison. And he said, 'Report these things to James and the brothers.' Then he left and went to another place." (Acts 12:6–17)

MINISTRIES

CHAPTER 16

THE WORSHIPING MINISTRY

"In the year of King Uzziah's death I saw the Lord sitting on a throne, high and lifted up, with the train of His robe filling the temple. Seraphim stood above Him, each having six wings: with two he covered his face, and with two he covered his feet, and with two he flew. And one called out to another and said,

'Holy, Holy, Holy, is Yahweh of hosts;

The whole earth is full of His glory.'

"And the foundations of the thresholds shook at the voice of him who called out, while the house of God was filling with smoke." (Isaiah 6:1–4)

Ayin

GABRIEL: And now let us discuss the various tasks which Yahweh has created us angels to carry out for Him.

MICHAEL: We are so privileged to serve the Holy One in all these manners.

GABRIEL: First and of the utmost priority comes the avenue of worshipping Yahweh and leading others to do likewise.

MICHAEL: Through this means, we give the appropriate honor and exaltation to the King of all creation.

GABRIEL: Collectively we recite back to Him all His wonderful perfections, such His being all-knowing, all-wise, all-powerful, and everywhere present.

MICHAEL: We ascribe to Yahweh the glory to His name: holy, righteous, just, as well as good, kind, benevolent, gracious, loving, and merciful.

GABRIEL: We extol His perfections of sovereignty, truthfulness, faithfulness, and self-existence.

MICHAEL: His essence expresses Himself as being altogether lovely and worthy of every means of recognition.

GABRIEL: There is validation for this purpose when the writer of Hebrews states: "when He again brings the firstborn into the world, He says, "Let all the angels of God worship Him." (Hebrews 1:6)

MICHAEL: Further description may be found in Yahweh's revelation to John:

"And all the angels were standing around the throne, and around the elders and the four living creatures, and they fell on their faces before the throne and worshiped God, saying, 'Amen, the blessings and the glory and the wisdom and the thanksgiving and the honor and the power and the strength, be to our God forever and ever. Amen.' " (Revelation 7:11–12)

GABRIEL: There is no doubt that we are to constantly carry out this exercise of adoration for Him who alone is worthy.

MICHAEL: Yahweh deserves worship for who He is, and not only for this, but also for all that He does.

GABRIEL: His activities emanate from who He is in essence, further demonstrating His excellencies.

MICHAEL: For example, His goodness toward all His creation comes about because of everything He personifies in His core. He is good Himself.

GABRIEL: And the same may be said of Yahweh's love, justice, benevolence, and graciousness. The reason we experience these qualities may be traced to His intrinsic perfection.

MICHAEL: Therefore, our worship extends not only to who He is, but also for everything He does.

GABRIEL: Obviously then, there can be no end to the reasons we worship the only eternal King and only wise God!

MICHAEL: Hereby we provide the perfect example for mankind as to how they are to satisfactorily respond to the Almighty.

GABRIEL: Yes, they have the opportunity to join us at every juncture.

"Then I looked, and I heard the voice of many angels around the throne and the living creatures and the elders; and the number of them was myriads of myriads, and thousands of thousands, saying with a loud voice,

'Worthy is the Lamb that was slain to receive power and riches and wisdom and strength and honor and glory and blessing.'

"And every created thing which is in heaven and on the earth and under the earth and on the sea, and all things in them, I heard saying,

" 'To Him who sits on the throne, and to the Lamb, be the blessing and the honor and the glory and the might forever and ever.'

"And the four living creatures kept saying, 'Amen.' And the elders fell down and worshiped." (Revelation 5:11–14)

CHAPTER 17

THE PRAISING MINISTRY

"Praise Yah!
Praise Yahweh from the heavens;
Praise Him in the heights!
Praise Him, all His angels;
Praise Him, all His hosts!
Praise Him, sun and moon;
Praise Him, all stars of light!
Praise Him, heavens of heavens,
And the waters that are above the heavens!
Let them praise the name of Yahweh,
For He commanded and they were created.
He caused them to stand forever and ever;
He gave a statute and it will never pass away.

"Praise Yahweh from the earth,
Sea monsters and all deeps;
Fire and hail, snow and clouds;

Stormy wind, doing His word;

Mountains and all hills;

Fruit trees and all cedars;

Beasts and all cattle;

Creeping things and winged bird;

Kings of the earth and all peoples;

Princes and all judges of the earth;

Both choice men as well as virgins;

The old with the young.

"Let them praise the name of Yahweh,

For His name alone is set on high;

His splendor is above earth and heaven.

And He has raised up a horn for His people,

Praise for all His holy ones;

For the sons of Israel, a people near to Him.

Praise Yah!" (Psalm 148:1–14)

Pe

MICHAEL: Shall we now interact about another closely related ministry: praising the Most High?

GABRIEL: There is no doubt that as angels we are called to give praise to our gracious King. Therefore, let us clarify the parameters of this important ministry.

MICHAEL: To be clear, we praise the Almighty when we declare who He is or what He has done.

GABRIEL: And He has so many excellencies which may be proclaimed, that this, of course, never need end.

MICHAEL: When we consider all His works, there is not enough time to enumerate them all.

GABRIEL: Wonderful Yahweh always must be honored before every audience.

MICHAEL: Praising clearly is distinguished from worship.

GABRIEL: Yes, praise and worship are distinct, whereas in worship we address our words to Yahweh Himself, and in praise we tell others of His greatness.

MICHAEL: It may be described as bragging on God to others.

GABRIEL: And with men, this act always must be public and vocal.

MICHAEL: Many times, praise comes as a fulfillment of a vow or promise to do so.

GABRIEL: In addition, the expression *hallelujah* is a promise or challenge to praise.

MICHAEL: Just saying the word does not accomplish the intent, but rather telling who Yahweh is or what He has done it is the act of giving praise.

GABRIEL: We angels have had many occasions throughout history to employ praise.

MICHAEL: Whereas all of Yahweh's creation fulfills this purpose even without a word in ways difficult to explain.

GABRIEL: Even the whisper of the wind announces His kindness.

MICHAEL: Or the roar of a young lion declares His power.

GABRIEL: Psalm 19 points to these truths when it says:

> "The heavens are telling of the glory of God;
> And the expanse is declaring the work of His hands.
> Day to day pours forth speech,

And night to night reveals knowledge.
There is no speech, nor are there words;
Their voice is not heard." (Psalm 19:1–3)

MICHAEL: The apostle Paul describes this more fully:

"That which is known about God is evident within them; for God made it evident to them. For since the creation of the world His invisible attributes, both His eternal power and divine nature, have been clearly seen, being understood through what has been made, so that they are without excuse." (Romans 1:19–20)

GABRIEL: All of creation clearly shows who Yahweh is and what He has done.

MICHAEL: Returning to our earlier statements, angels most definitely perform this noble task.

GABRIEL: Maybe most memorably demonstrated at the birth of Jesus, when so much of Yahweh's essence was communicated by His angels.

"And suddenly there appeared with the angel a multitude of the heavenly host praising God and saying, 'Glory to God in the highest, and on earth peace among men with whom He is pleased.'" (Luke 2:13–14)

MICHAEL: We have often been sent to deliver this function for the benefit of humans and really all of creation.

GABRIEL: There can never be too much praise of our awesome King of the universe! After all, we're called upon to bless Yahweh :

> "Bless Yahweh, you His angels,
> Mighty in strength, who perform His word,
> Obeying the voice of His word!
> Bless Yahweh, all you His hosts,
> You who serve Him, doing His will.
> Bless Yahweh, all you works of His,
> In all places of His rule;
> Bless Yahweh, O my soul!." (Psalm 103:20–22)

GABRIEL: What an honor to be responsible for this task!

MICHAEL: To magnify His majestic splendor gives us immeasurable pleasure and meaning.

GABRIEL: Yahweh is so worthy of it all!

"After these things I heard something like a loud voice of a great crowd in heaven, saying,

'Hallelujah! Salvation and glory and power belong to our God; because His judgments are true and righteous; for He has judged the great harlot who was corrupting the earth with her sexual immorality, and He has avenged the blood of His slaves shed by her hand.' . . . And the twenty-four elders and the four living creatures fell down and worshiped God who sits on the throne saying, 'Amen. Hallelujah!' And a voice came from the throne, saying,

'Give praise to our God, all you His slaves, you who fear Him, the small and the great.' " (Revelation 19:1–2, 4–5)

CHAPTER 18

THE INFORMING MINISTRY

"Then I saw another angel flying in midheaven, having an eternal gospel to proclaim to those who inhabit the earth, and to every nation and tribe and tongue and people. And he said with a loud voice, 'Fear God, and give Him glory, because the hour of His judgment has come; worship Him who made the heaven and the earth and sea and springs of waters.'" (Revelation 14:6–7)

Y

Tsadhe

GABRIEL: The next ministry for us to discuss is informing, which includes proclaiming, directing, and encouraging.

MICHAEL: There have been numerous occasions where this was the mission we were sent out to accomplish.

GABRIEL: You remember when Yahweh accompanied us to meet with Abraham regarding the grievous sin of Sodom and Gomorrah?

MICHAEL: As Yahweh disclosed to Abraham what He was about to do with them, we went to Sodom to see for ourselves.

GABRIEL: Undoubtedly, we found out as the men sought to abuse us sexually, which prompted us to strike them with blindness.

MICHAEL: Then we said to Lot, "Whom else have you here? A son-in-law, and your sons, and your daughters, and everyone you have in the city, bring *them* out of the place; for we are about to destroy this place because their outcry has become great before Yahweh, so Yahweh has sent us to destroy it." (Genesis 19:12–13)

GABRIEL: In this way we let Lot and his family know God's intent and directed them how to avoid being swept away in this judgment.

MICHAEL: We were very clear about what they needed to do.

GABRIEL: Another occasion where we were instrumental in explaining Yahweh's activities involved Daniel.

MICHAEL: This event stands out because as Daniel was weighed down with so much to take place in the future, we were sent to let him know what was taking place behind the scenes.

GABRIEL: Daniel was "appalled at what had appeared, and there was none to make [him] understand it." And so he entreated Yahweh with much humility and repentance for God's anger and wrath to be turned away from Israel. (Daniel 8:22–9:19)

MICHAEL: As he was entreating for the mercy of the King, you were sent in response to clarify Yahweh's position.

GABRIEL: I made him understand and spoke to him saying. "O Daniel, I have now come forth to give you insight and understanding. At the beginning of your supplications the word was issued, so I have come to tell you, for you are highly esteemed; so understand the message and gain understanding in what has appeared." (Daniel 9:22–23)

MICHAEL: Then you gave him a more detailed explanation: "and the word was true and one of great conflict, but he understood the word and had understanding of what had appeared." (Daniel 10:1)

GABRIEL: Nevertheless Daniel mourned for three weeks, and so I appeared again in a vision. I reassured him: "O Daniel, man of high esteem, understand the words that I am about to speak to you. . . Do not be afraid, Daniel, for from the first day that you gave your heart to understand *this* and to humble yourself before your God, your words were heard, and I have come *in response* to your words." (10:11–12)

MICHAEL: And then the Glorious One instructed you to make him understand the vision and then you went on to explain the spiritual battle we were engaged in.

GABRIEL: Absolutely! I told him that the prince of the kingdom of Persia, a fallen angel, had withstood me twenty-one days, but that you, Michael, being one of the chief princes, had come to help me, for I alone had faced this demon. (10:13)

MICHAEL: Thus, I had come to relieve you of this duty so that you could go communicate all this to God's servant, Daniel.

GABRIEL: Then I made him stand up after he had fallen on his face in a deep sleep. And I said, "Now I have come to give you an understanding of what will happen to your people in the last days, for the vision pertains to the days yet future" (Daniel 10:14). After I had renewed

his failing strength, I consoled him one more time saying: "O man of high esteem, do not be afraid. Peace be with you; gather strength and be strong!" (10:19)

MICHAEL: So, this strengthened him to be able to handle more truth from you.

GABRIEL: I reminded him as to why I had come to him and proceeded to let him know that I would return to fight against the demon over Persia. Also, my going back would also trigger the demon over Greece to engage in battle as well. (10:20)

MICHAEL: Therefore, you promised to tell Daniel what is inscribed in the book of truth.

GABRIEL: I concluded by clarifying that only you, Michael, as their steadfast prince over them, contends by my side (10:21). After that I indicated the meaning of the vision and told him to "seal up the book until the time of the end." (Daniel 12:4)

MICHAEL: As we have talked about previously, this is just so important that let us rehearse it again. Hundreds of years later, you and I were instrumental in conveying monumental messages to Zachariah, Mary, and Joseph.

GABRIEL: In preparation for the most significant event soon to take place on earth, we were called upon to announce Yahweh's statements about the future.

MICHAEL: First you appeared to Zachariah, a Levitical priest, as he served in the temple.

GABRIEL: I stood on the right side of the altar of incense when Zachariah came to burn the incense. And here I disclosed to him the son he and Elizabeth, his wife, would have.

MICHAEL: Describe his response.

GABRIEL: He was troubled, and fear fell upon him, and the message I spoke to him only confused him further.

MICHAEL: Your pronouncement clarified that his wife would have a child even though she was old and barren.

GABRIEL: I gave him a detailed explanation regarding his son. How he was to be named John and to be raised according to the plan.

MICHAEL: He doubted how this could take place.

GABRIEL: This is when I told him, "I am Gabriel, who stands before God, and I was sent to speak to you and to bring you this good news." (Luke 1:19)

MICHAEL: Because of his lack of faith, you rendered him mute until the birth took place.

GABRIEL: Correct. And then I was instructed to also proclaim to Mary, who was a virgin promised to marry Joseph, a man from the line of King David, that she would be with child.

MICHAEL: Describe how this took place.

GABRIEL: I said, "Greetings, favored one! The Lord is with you." Mary was greatly perplexed at this salutation, and fear came up in her. (1:28–29)

MICHAEL: Again, this is not surprising since our huge and glowing appearance tends to overwhelm humans.

GABRIEL: Absolutely. Consequently, I sought to calm her fears by saying, "Do not be afraid, Mary, for you have found favor with God." (1:30)

MICHAEL: Then you went on to describe the point of your visit, right?

GABRIEL: I told her she would conceive in her womb and bear a son and call His name Jesus and described His significance.

MICHAEL: What was it that Mary replied to you?

GABRIEL: She asked, "How will this be, since I am a virgin?" (1:34). Which is a perfectly logical inquiry.

MICHAEL: How did you explain the process involved?

GABRIEL: I responded just as Yahweh instructed me: "The Holy Spirit will come upon you, and the power of the Most High will overshadow you; and for that reason the holy Child shall be called the Son of God." (1:35)

MICHAEL: It was at that time that you related what was taking place with her relative, Elizabeth right?

GABRIEL: I informed her that Elizabeth was miraculously going to deliver a child as well.

MICHAEL: Mary's reaction was truly amazing!

GABRIEL: Surely it was. She said, "Behold, the slave of the Lord; may it be done to me according to your word" (1:38). This response could have only come by the power of the Holy Spirit.

MICHAEL: This was not an expected human reply.

GABRIEL: I was thrilled completely and departed her company.

MICHAEL: And then it was my opportunity to inform her betrothed as to what all was happening here.

GABRIEL: I am sure Joseph was conflicted by the pregnancy of Mary as he knew this did not occur because of him. He had remained pure toward her.

MICHAEL: Of course, as a righteous man and not wanting to publicly humiliate Mary, he made up his mind to divorce her privately. And that is when I appeared to him in a dream. (Matthew 1:19–20)

GABRIEL: This must have been very consoling to him with all this predicament swirling around him.

MICHAEL: I clearly told him to not be afraid to take Mary as his wife, for the conception was from the Holy Spirit.

GABRIEL: Yahweh's plan is always above reproach!

MICHAEL: I described that she would have a son and told him he was to call His name Jesus, for He will save His people from their sins. (1:21)

GABRIEL: This redemption is perfectly encapsulated in His name, which means "Yahweh saves."

MICHAEL: Names always carry such significance. Joseph received the message faithfully and responded in obedience to proceed with making Mary his wife.

GABRIEL: And he kept the conception pure by not having sex with her until after the baby Jesus was born.

MICHAEL: How wonderful it is to be used as a messenger of such importance!

GABRIEL: I always have such a sense of satisfaction when Yahweh allows me to carry out the tasks for which I was created.

MICHAEL: This revelation to Joseph was the missing piece in this scenario.

GABRIEL: Now Joseph and Mary would be a united front against the accusations, many of which would certainly be hurled their way.

MICHAEL: Absolutely! It proves to be the best when aligned with the Almighty One.

MICHAEL: This clearly concludes the long-awaited prophecy of the God-man coming to save mankind from their sin.

GABRIEL: The entrance was spectacular when you appeared to some shepherds out in the fields watching over their flock by night.

MICHAEL: Yahweh permitted His glory to shine through me, and so it was no wonder that along with the size of my body, they were filled with fear.

GABRIEL: We are familiar with this response, and so we seek first to comfort them.

MICHAEL: In fact, the first words I spoke were. "Do not be afraid; for behold, I bring you good news of great joy which will be for all the people." (Luke 2:10)

GABRIEL: I am sure this relieved their fears.

MICHAEL: And then I explained that the news was filled with great joy for all the people.

GABRIEL: What an apt description!

MICHAEL: I continued, "For today in the city of David there has been born for you a Savior, who is Christ the Lord" (2:11). Next, I told them how to find Him.

GABRIEL: The sign for them was they would find a baby wrapped in swaddling clothes and lying in a manger, right?

MICHAEL: Yes. Consequently they knew to be looking for a place with animals.

GABRIEL: While the shepherds were contemplating all these words, the multitude of other angels joined me, and we were all praising God.

MICHAEL: We said, "Glory to God in the highest, and on earth peace among men, with whom He is pleased." (2:14)

GABRIEL: When we were departed from their presence, they made their way over to the stable nearby in Bethlehem.

MICHAEL: Subsequently they found Mary and Joseph in a stable, and the baby Jesus lying in a feeding trough. (2:16)

GABRIEL: And when they related the pronouncement you declared to them, they all wondered at these events.

MICHAEL: Meanwhile, Mary treasured up all these things, pondering them in her heart. (2:19)

GABRIEL: The shepherds then returned with magnanimous adoration to Yahweh, and telling others what He had done, just as they had heard and seen from us.

MICHAEL: The wonder of it all and the joy of recounting the splendor of Yahweh's wisdom and grace!

GABRIEL: How glorious it was and is to be instruments of our King to relay His good news to humans!

"Then one of the seven angels who have the seven bowls full of the seven last plagues came and spoke with me, saying, 'Come here, I will show you the bride, the wife of the Lamb.' And he carried me away in the Spirit to a great and high mountain, and showed me the holy city, Jerusalem, coming down out of heaven from God." (Revelation 21:9–10)

CHAPTER 19

THE SERVING MINISTRY

"And of the angels He says, 'Who makes His angels winds, And His ministers flaming fire.' . . . Are they not all ministering spirits, sent to render service for the sake of those who will inherit salvation?" (Hebrews 1:7, 14)

ר

Qoph

MICHAEL: And now we come to a much more general category of ministry: serving.

GABRIEL: Obviously, everything we do could be considered serving, for that is who we are.

MICHAEL: Job used some very descriptive terms which help to depict this activity.

GABRIEL: Here we are noted as "presenting ourselves before Yahweh."

MICHAEL: This phrase conveys the concept of making ourselves available to do Yahweh's bidding—whatever that may be.

GABRIEL: Thus, we offer ourselves to carry out His missions.

MICHAEL: In fact, for this purpose, we were created by the Master to do His will as He commands.

GABRIEL: Sometimes we are sent just to speak a word to one of His servants, like the prophet Zachariah.

MICHAEL: Zachariah describes Joshua, the high priest, as being "clothed with filthy garments." (Zachariah 3:3)

GABRIEL: Then, the angel of Yahweh, Jesus, asked us to clothe Joshua with pure garments. (3:5)

MICHAEL: Thus, we appropriately provided him with clean vestments, holy to God.

GABRIEL: This provides but one small example of tasks we angels are called upon in serving Yahweh.

MICHAEL: Furthermore, we are "all ministering spirits sent to render service for the sake of those who will? inherit salvation." (Hebrews 1:14)

GABRIEL: John conveys the relationship various angels have in a service capacity over specific early churches in Revelation 2:1, 8, 12, 18; 3:1, 7, 14.

MICHAEL: Not only in the last book of the Scriptures is this activity communicated but also in the first book.

GABRIEL: In Genesis 28 when Jacob (now known as Israel) was on his way to Haran, he saw in a dream angels ascending to heaven as well as descending to earth, carrying out His service.

MICHAEL: Since we are named angels, which means messengers, of course, we are always in the service of Yahweh. And in the business of accomplishing our assigned tasks.

GABRIEL: The measure of our satisfaction in being used by Yahweh to fulfill His purposes is so immense!

MICHAEL: What greater sense of significance than to be involved in Yahweh's perfect design?

⁓

"Bless Yahweh, you His angels,
Mighty in strength, who perform His word,
Obeying the voice of His word!
Bless Yahweh, all you His hosts,
You who serve Him, doing His will.
Bless Yahweh, all you works of His,
In all places of His rule;
Bless Yahweh, O my soul!" (Psalm 103:20–22)

CHAPTER 20

THE PROTECTING MINISTRY

"For He will command His angels concerning you,
To guard you in all your ways.
On their hands they will bear you up,
Lest you strike your foot against a stone." (Psalm 91:11–12)

ר

Resh

GABRIEL: Let us take some time to entertain another major category of our ministry: protecting God's creation.

MICHAEL: Clearly Yahweh has used us to put a hedge of defense around His people and, in fact, over all that He has made.

GABRIEL: A prime example of this calling may be seen in our intervention on behalf of Lot and his family.

MICHAEL: This care was given to Lot because of his being the nephew of Abraham who was favored by Yahweh.

GABRIEL: The area Lot chose to tend his flocks was at that time very fertile and attractive, like the Garden of Eden. (Genesis 13:11)

MICHAEL: True, but unfortunately inhabited by very ungodly people as well.

GABRIEL: Yahweh had heard the outcries concerning these wicked people's actions, and so we went with the angel of Yahweh (Jesus) to verify all this for ourselves.

MICHAEL: Due to their association, we went first to Abraham, God's man.

GABRIEL: Abraham realized immediately he was entertaining representatives from heaven above and showed us extreme hospitality. (Genesis 18)

MICHAEL: He encouraged our delay by first bringing water to wash our feet and then provided food and drink to refresh us along the way. (18:4)

GABRIEL: Part of our mission included clarifying that Abraham's wife, Sarah, would bear a son in a year to their disbelief. (18:10)

MICHAEL: They had trouble accepting this, even though Yahweh had promised this for many years.

GABRIEL: They both were approaching one hundred years of age and let their physical limitations restrict their faith.

MICHAEL: This miracle stretched their faith as well as the interaction regarding Lot.

GABRIEL: Yahweh had contemplated as to whether to share His plans and concluded this should not be hidden from His faithful servant. (18:17–18)

MICHAEL: Jesus described the situation in Sodom and delineated His plan to visit for verification before bringing judgment.

GABRIEL: We were seen as men because we had taken on human bodies to meet with the people involved.

MICHAEL: You and I then headed down to Sodom while Jesus continued this discussion with Abraham.

GABRIEL: Abraham then proceeded to plead with Yahweh to spare the inhabitants. He asked Yahweh to spare it if only fifty were found to be righteous and then forty-five, forty, thirty, twenty, and finally ten. (18:23–33)

MICHAEL: Yahweh agreed to each number and went His way when He had finished speaking with Abraham.

GABRIEL: Meanwhile, when we arrived in Sodom it was evening and Lot was sitting in the gate of the town. (Genesis 19:1)

MICHAEL: He greeted us with the same hospitality as Abraham since he recognized we were sent by the Almighty.

GABRIEL: He quickly invited us to lodge with his family, although we tried to refuse. (19:2)

MICHAEL: But sensing the danger, Lot persisted strongly, and we finally agreed.

GABRIEL: After he provided a luxurious meal, we prepared to sleep for the night but were interrupted by all the men of the town at the door. (19:4)

MICHAEL: Their cry was for these new men to be brought out so that they could have sexual relations with us. (19:5)

GABRIEL: Lot attempted to dissuade them but when they sought to break down the door, we intervened by first pulling Lot inside, then securing the door. (19:10)

MICHAEL: Then we blinded them so that they could not find their way, and they left off pursuing us. (19:11)

GABRIEL: At this point we asked if there were others associated with him and let them know we would take them out of this place. (19:12)

MICHAEL: We made it clear that we were about to destroy Sodom because of the evil outcry against its people.

GABRIEL: As morning dawned, we urged Lot to take his wife and daughters and get out so as not to be swept away in the impending destruction. (19:15)

MICHAEL: Since they tarried, we grabbed them by the hand which indicated Yahweh was being merciful to them and forcefully took them outside the town. (9:16)

GABRIEL: Then you told them to escape for their life and not look back in the valley at the punishment administered. (9:17)

MICHAEL: Despite the exhortation for them to flee to the hills, Lot thanked us for the great kindness in saving his life but asked to be allowed to go to a nearby small town. (19:19–20)

GABRIEL: You granted his request and urged expediency since we couldn't do anything until they were safe. (19:22)

MICHAEL: When Lot came to Zoar Yahweh commenced to rain down sulfur and fire upon Sodom and Gomorrah out of heaven. (19:24)

GABRIEL: This destroyed the city, its people, all the valley and scorched the ground as well. No longer was this a fertile valley.

MICHAEL: Unfortunately, Lots' wife didn't heed our warning and upon looking back became a pillar of salt. (19:26)

GABRIEL: Meanwhile, Abraham arose early in the morning, and as he looked down, he saw all the valley filled with smoke like that of a furnace.

MICHAEL: "Thus it happened, when God destroyed the cities of the valley, that God remembered Abraham and sent Lot out of the midst of the overthrow, when He overthrew the cities in which Lot lived." (19:29)

GABRIEL: In addition, I would be remiss if I did not bring up the instance with Daniel and the lion's den and how we shut their mouths.

MICHAEL: His companions Shadrach, Meshach, and Abednego, who were kept from even the smell of the fire in their clothing from the overheating furnace. (Daniel 3:27)

GABRIEL: One final mention goes to our myriads being revealed to the prophet Elisha's servant.

MICHAEL: His servant had only been able to see the massive Syrian Army which physically surrounded them until Elisha prayed that Yahweh would open his servant's spiritual eyes to see all of us outnumbering the Syrians by far. (2 Kings 6:17)

GABRIEL: Therefore, we had been there all along, protecting the man of God who was being attacked.

MICHAEL: Thus, there are many times when men see only the physical surroundings and miss the spiritual realms which are about them.

GABRIEL: Most of the time when we are sent on missions, we are undetected by humans.

MICHAEL: Yahweh always has in mind to guard all His creatures.

GABRIEL: And without question, He uses us angels to help prevent anything detrimental to His plan.

MICHAEL: Yahweh undoubtedly seeks the best for His subjects in whatever way most suits Him.

GABRIEL: He always knows the ultimate plan to bring about His wonderful design.

MICHAEL: The fact that Yahweh often uses us to accomplish His purpose, brings extreme satisfaction!

GABRIEL: May He always be praised for His glorious works which demonstrate His divine perfections!

"This grace was given, to proclaim to the Gentiles the good news of the unfathomable riches of Christ, and to bring to light for all what is the administration of the mystery which for ages has been hidden in God who created all things; so that the manifold wisdom of God might now be made known through the church to the rulers and the authorities in the heavenly places." (Ephesians 3:8–10)

CHAPTER 21

THE ENFORCING MINISTRY

"After these things I looked, and the sanctuary of the tabernacle of testimony in heaven was opened, and the seven angels who have the seven plagues came out of the sanctuary, clothed in linen, clean and bright, and girded around their chests with golden sashes. Then one of the four living creatures gave to the seven angels seven golden bowls full of the wrath of God, who lives forever and ever. And the sanctuary was filled with smoke from the glory of God and from His power; and no one was able to enter the sanctuary until the seven plagues of the seven angels were finished." (Revelation 15:5–8)

Sin/ Shin

MICHAEL: While all the ministries of angels up to this point have been to encourage and benefit mankind, this last discourse reveals another relevant perspective to Yahweh.

GABRIEL: His love, grace, and forbearance may be emphasized by humans because of the pleasant results which resound to them.

MICHAEL: However, the excellencies of Yahweh, which may come across as more negative, are just as true and important.

GABRIEL: Rooted in His hate for and separation from sin, which we call holiness, come the qualities of righteousness and justice.

MICHAEL: As a holy being who is completely perfect, the judgements He dispenses are therefore true and just.

GABRIEL: Just like with Yahweh's other perfections, He may not deny this side of Himself. All of His perfections are equally true and certain.

MICHAEL: And so, the punishment He brings upon His creation perfectly fits the unsavory actions which prompted them.

GABRIEL: Unquestionably, His judgments provide an appropriate response to those things that are anathema to Him.

MICHAEL: In most cases, Yahweh's wrath has already been stalled by His mercy and longsuffering!

GABRIEL: Consider the story already recounted of Sodom and Gomorrah.

MICHAEL: When we first visited Abraham, Yahweh informed him of His plan to consider the wickedness of Lot's city.

GABRIEL: And then we were sent to be Yahweh's feet on the ground.

MICHAEL: We ascertained after nearly being accosted ourselves by the evil men of the town that God's punishment on them was just.

GABRIEL: Yahweh used us to physically remove Lot, his wife, and his daughters, and then He rained down sulfur and fire on the area.

MICHAEL: Thus, we were used in this instance to carry out the Almighty's judgment on these people.

GABRIEL: Then there are other cases when we are commanded to inflict retribution on those who oppose God's people.

MICHAEL: Sometimes just our presence was enough to deter their enemies, as it was when Elijah and his servant were surrounded by a huge Syrian army of 185,000.

GABRIEL: Elijah calmed his servant from being overwhelmed with fear.

MICHAEL: He prayed that Yahweh would open his servants' eyes and when he did, the young man became aware that we were more numerous and, in fact, the mountain surrounding was full of our horses and chariots of fire. (2 Kings 6:15–17)

GABRIEL: The lesson learned was that just because we may not be visible to the physical eye, this does not mean that we are not always present and available to defend.

MICHAEL: Most of the instances when we are carrying out the righteous judgments of Yahweh are described in John's Revelation.

GABRIEL: Yes, but Jude also clearly depicts a summary of these activities when he quotes Enoch: "Behold, the Lord came with many thousands of His holy ones, to execute judgment upon all, and to convict all the ungodly of all their deeds of ungodliness which they have done in an ungodly way." (Jude 14–15)

MICHAEL: John paints a vivid picture of how we were called into action to dispense the wrath of Yahweh.

GABRIEL: There are four of us standing on the four corners of the earth, holding back any wind that might destroy creation. (Revelation 7:1)

MICHAEL: This harm will be restrained until the 144,000 Israeli servants have the seal on their foreheads.

GABRIEL: And when the Lamb opens the seventh seal, then seven of us standing before the King are given trumpets to blow, each commencing a different destruction upon the earth. (8:6)

MICHAEL: Each of the catastrophes are unleashed, one by one, bringing death and judgment upon the earth and its inhabitants.

GABRIEL: What surprises me the most is that even with these tumultuous calamities, man does not repent of their evil.

MICHAEL: And consequently, Yahweh continues with His exacting punishments.

GABRIEL: This is carried out to the point that sickles were given to two of us to reap the harvest of the earth, to be thrown into the winepress of the wrath of God. (14:15–19)

MICHAEL: And that is not all, for seven more angels come equipped with seven plagues to finish the wrath of Yahweh. (15:1)

GABRIEL: These golden bowls are given to pour out upon the earth, sea, rivers and sun fire, darkness, shriveling, lightnings, rumblings, peals of thunder, and a giant earthquake like none before plus one-hundred-pound hailstones!

MICHAEL: After this purging, we summon the birds of the air to come feast upon all those destroyed by these plagues. (19:21)

GABRIEL: Ultimately, then, we angels usher in the new heavenly Jerusalem to its location now upon the earth.

MICHAEL: In all His grandeur, the Almighty will reign, and His glory will be the light source for the city. (21:23)

GABRIEL: Which is just as it was in the beginning, before the sun, moon, and stars were created.

MICHAEL: And the water of life will flow from His throne to water the twelve types of the tree of life, each yielding its fruit each month.

GABRIEL: No longer will there be anything accursed, but the throne of God and of the Lamb will be in it.

MICHAEL: And all His servants will worship Him forever!

GABRIEL: Then we will all reign with Yahweh forever and ever, amen!

MICHAEL: Glory be to the Father, and to the Son, and to the Holy Spirit;
As it was in the beginning, is now, and ever shall be:

GABRIEL: World without end, Amen and Amen!

"I, Jesus, sent My angel to bear witness to you of these things for the churches. I am the root and the descendant of David, the bright morning star." And the Spirit and the bride say, 'Come.' And let the one who hears say, 'Come.' And let the one who is thirsty come. Let the one who wishes receive the water of life without cost." (Revelation 22:16–17)

ADDENDUM

THE NATURE OF AND FACTS ABOUT ANGELS

Tav

1. Angels all were created at the beginning of time.

2. Angel's have a purpose to carry out Yahweh's will.

3. Angels are spirit beings and therefore sexless, although they always have male names and are seen physically as men.

4. They do not have bodies, although they may assume one.

5. They do not propagate but are a set number.

6. They number hundreds of millions.

7. They do not die and thus their quantity is fixed.

8. They are not glorified human beings.

9. Humans cannot become angels when they die.

10.   They are not intended to be worshipped.

11.   They do not require food for sustenance.

12.   They are holy, that is separated unto God from sin for special purposes.

13.   They are elect, that is chosen by God for the accomplishments of Divine ends.

14.   They are not redeemed (the unfallen) nor redeemable (the fallen).

15.   They are a created order and not demigods.

16.   They were created by the beginning of the third day.

17.   They were all created simultaneously and immediately.

18.   They appear to be divided into various orders, i.e., rulers, authorities, powers, dominions, etc.

19.   They have at least one archangel: Michael.

20.   They have at least one mighty one: Gabriel.

21.   They have among them cherubim, guardians of holiness.

22.   They have among them seraphim, fiery agents for cleansing.

23.   They have among them angels of judgment: Abaddon or Apollyon.

24.   They will continue into eternity.

25.   They include fallen (unclean) ones who serve Satan and continually seek to destroy the plans of Yahweh.

ANGELOLOGY

GENERAL ANGELOLOGY

Richard Mant (177fr1848)

Having considered God as the Creator and Provident Ruler of the universe we must now give attention to the two chief orders of his creation--angels and men. Mankind will be studied extensively in Part Four. Also, since God has chosen in some instances to use angels as agents of his providence, it is in order to consider them at this point

The Bible does not present what might be called a formal doctrine of angels. Furthermore, when compared to the other major heads of theology this doctrine certainly ranks far down on the list. "The angelic world is but a secondary theme throughout the Bible; scripture concentrates instead on the incomparable glory of Yahweh and on the wonder of his provision of redemption for fallen mankind" (Carl F. H. Henry, <u>God, Revelation and Authority,</u> VI, 231). Nonetheless, there is a sizable amount of data in the Bible relating to spirit beings which must be considered if we are to understand certain other truths (e.g., the doctrines of sin; the world; the Christian life).

The biblical approach to this subject should be as instructive to us as is the doctrine itself. We are given the essential information needed but no more. No room is given for wild speculation or fanciful extensions beyond the basics. Henry points out the care with which scripture approaches this subject:

> This paucity of reference to angels reinforces what is characteristic of biblical religion: unlike many non-biblical religions its primary focus is on the living God in the invisible spirit world, and on man in the created universe.... Unlike the polytheistic setting of the ancient near East that teems with pagan notions of the world of invisible demigods and demons, the Old Testament speaks primarily of the centrality of the one true God and only very secondarily of life in the invisible heavenly realms. Yahweh is the one and only creative causality in the universe and in history. There is no room for strange philosophical and religious notions of transient emanations or aeons such as the Gnostics asserted (op. cit., p. 231-32).

I. Introduction

A. Development of the Doctrine in Church History

Throughout the history of the church the doctrine of angels has suffered intermittently from inordinate preoccupation and inordinate neglect. Some treatments have been wildly speculative while others, especially in modern times, have viewed such a doctrine ftas a relic of a prescientific and uncritical way of thinking" (Millard Erickson, <u>Christian Theology.</u> I, 434). In the second century Justin Martyr included angels among those beings whom Christians should worship <u>(Apology.</u> 1.6). Thomas Aquinas in his <u>Summa Theologica,</u> and other works, gave extensive attention to angels. In contrast, in this century Rudolf Bultmann has completely explained away the existence of a spirit world through his demythologizing hermeneutic (see e.g., "New Testament and Mythology," in <u>Kerygma and Myth,</u> Hans Bartsch, editor, p. 5). As far as demons are concerned Karl Barth held that ftthe origin and nature of demons lie in nothingness, chaos, darkness" (Erickson, op. cit., p. 447; see Karl Barth, <u>Church Dogmatics,</u> III/3, 523). Erickson goes on to note, They are not created by God, but are part of the threat to God's creation" (ibid.). Paul Tillich held that angels are nothing more than "concrete-poetic symbols of the structures or powers of being. They are not beings.

. . ." (<u>Systematic Theology,</u> I, 260). (See Louis Berkhof, <u>Systematic Theology,</u> pp. 141-43 for a more extended treatment.)

B. Meaning and Use of the Word "Angel"

1. <u>Meaning</u> The Hebrew word for angel is <u>mal'ak</u> and the Greek term is <u>angelos.</u> They both mean one who brings a message; a messenger.

2. <u>Usage</u> The term usually refers to created spirit beings. Sometimes in the Old Testament, however, it probably refers to the second person of the Godhead (see below III A 4) and on a few occasions the term is used of men as messengers (for example 1 Kings 19:20; Matt. 11:10, John the Baptist; Luke 7:24; 9:52; James 2:25; Rev. 2:1, 8, 12, 18; 3:1, 7, 14). For the most part, when the word refers to spirits, the messenger is viewed as one who serves. On some occasions, at least, they are designated as "sons of God" (Job 1:6; 2:1; 38:7; and possibly Gen. 6:2, 4).

II. Their Order in Creation

A Their Origin

1. <u>The fact of their creation</u> is stated in Psalm 148:2-5 and Colossians 1:16. Note well that they are created beings and, therefore while they are not of the same created order as mankind neither are they demigods. *As with the entire creation they, too, are accountable to their Creator.*

2. <u>The time of their creation</u> was before the creation of the material world, Job 38:4-7. They do not seem, however, to have been created before the first day in light of Colossians 1:16 and Exodus 20:11, since all things are said to have been created <u>during</u> creation week (cf. Ps. 33:6). Thus it would appear that they were created at the beginning of the first day since they rejoiced over the creation of the earth.

3. <u>The entire angelic host was evidently created simultaneously</u> and immediately since they do not reproduce (Matt. 22:30). Note, too, that they are referred to as sons of God, but never as sons of angels.

B. Their Nature

1. <u>They are spirit beings</u> (Heb. 1:14).

2. <u>They are incorporeal</u> (Luke 24:39, cf. Heb. 1:14), although they can assume bodily form (Gen. 18:1-19:1).

3. <u>They do not propagate after their kind</u> (Matt. 22:30).

4. <u>They do not die</u> (Luke 20:36).

C. Their Number

They are innumerable (Heb. 12:22; Rev. 5:11) and since there is neither birth nor death the number seems to be fixed.

D. Their Rank

There is at least one archangel, Michael (Jude 9), while the angels are divided into various orders (for example: rulers. authorities, powers, dominions, etc.) (Eph. 1:21; 6:12; Col. 1:16; 2:15).

E. Their Relationship to Men

1. <u>They are not glorified human beings</u> as seen in Hebrews 12:22- 23 where they are distinguished from mankind. Note the <u>hos</u> ("as" or "like") in Matthew 22:30 and the <u>isangeloi</u> in Luke 20:36 (which should be understood as "like the angels" not "equal to angels"). Furthermore, they are above the sphere of men (Ps. 8:4-5, cf. Heb. 2:7) in the sense that they are pure spirit and thus of a different created order; they rejoice over the salvation of men (Luke 15:10); and they will be judged by the saints (1 Cor. 6:3) all of which distinguish them from human kind.

2. <u>They are not to be worshipped</u> (Col. 2:18; Rev. 19:9-10; 22:8- 9). Perhaps the passage which most pointedly distinguishes them from deity, and thus from any rightful worship, is Hebrews 1:5-2:9. This passage clearly establishes the superiority of Jesus Christ to angels.

3. <u>At least once they transported a soul to heaven</u> (Luke 16:22, cf. Jude 9).

4. <u>They are not omniscient but do have great knowledge</u> (2 Sam. 14:20, cf. Matt. 24:36; 1 Pet. 1:12).

5. <u>They are not omnipotent but do have great power</u> (Ps. 103:20, cf. 2 Pet. 2:11).

III. Their Classification

A. Unfallen Angels

1. <u>Their nature</u>

a)   They are holy, that is separated unto God and from sin for special purposes (Mark 8:38; Acts 10:22; Rev. 14:10).

b)   They are elect, that is chosen by God for the accomplishment of divine ends (1 Tim. 5:21).

c)   They are not redeemed (or, in the case of the fallen angels, redeemable) as is true of mankind (Heb. 2:16).

2. <u>Their abode</u>

Heaven, possibly the second heaven (the first being physical and the third the throne of God), is their abode (Heb. 12:22; Matt. 18:10; 22:30). Isaiah 14:12 and following seems to suggest that they live in a sphere lower than God's throne. In light of such passages as Job 38:7 and Revelation 12:4, 9, where angels are associated with stars, some have felt that they dwell in celestial abodes or have a similar relationship to those heavenly bodies that mankind has to earth (cf. Deut. 4:19; Isa. 34:4; Jer. 8:2 where "hosts of heaven" is used of stars with 1 Kings 22:19; Luke 2:13; Revelation 19:4 where it is used of angels and Psalm 148:1-6; Isa. 24:21-23; 40:26; Job 38:7 where it is used of both at once. See Erich Sauer, <u>The Dawn of World</u> <u>Redemption,</u> p. 28).

3. <u>Their ministry</u>

Many of the following functions of angels seem to reinforce and illustrate the idea that angels are agents of God's providence.

a)   They minister to the elect, even before salvation (Heb. 1:14; although "salvation" here could refer to final salvation and thus this would be a statement regarding the "guardian angel" concept).

b)   They minister in relation to the church. Particularly, they observe the order of authority practiced therein and learn of God's wisdom (1 Cor. 11:10; Eph. 3:10; 1 Pet. 1:12).

c)   They minister in relation to Israel. According to Daniel 12:1, Michael the archangel, "who stands guard over the sons of [Daniel's] people," has special concern for Israel. Also angels were present at the giving of the law (Acts 7:53; Gal. 3:19) and in the future will gather elect Israel at the time of Christ's second coming (Matt. 24:31).

d)   They care for children. This is intended as an indication of the Father's interest in and concern for children and therefore of the concern that we in turn should have (Matt. 18:10).

e)   They have special interest in the people of God. This is sometimes referred to with the phrase "guardian angel" (see Ps. 91:11). Among other things they protect and deliver (Gen. 19:10-11; 1 Kings 19:5; Dan. 3:28; 6:22; Acts 5:19; 12:7-11; cf. 2 Kings 6:16-17) and inform, direct and encourage them (Matt. 28:5-7; Acts 8:26; 27:23-24).

f)   They had and will have an extensive ministry to Christ: at birth (Luke 2:13); following the temptation (Matt. 4:11);at the ascension (Acts 1:10); at the rapture (1 Thess. 4:16); at the second coming (Matt. 25:31; 2 Thess. 1:7).

g)   They have a ministry to the nations (Dan. 10:10-11:1; 12:1). The precise nature of this work is difficult to ascertain but it may be an extension of the "guardian angel" concept. (Ephesians 6:12 seems to give the negative (evil) side of this truth.)

h)   They worship and serve God as He chooses (Ps. 148:2; Matt. 18:10; Luke 1:19, 26; Heb. 1:6; Rev. 5:11-12; cf. Ezek. 28:14) and sometimes function as instruments of his judgment (Gen. 19:12-13; 2 Sam. 24:16; 2 Kings 19:35; Ezek. 9:1; Matt. 13:36-42; 49-50; Acts 12:23; Rev. 7:2; 8:6-9:21; 16:4-17).

i)   They function as agents of praise (Rev. 4:6-9; 5:8-10; 5:11-12; 5:13-14; 7:11-12; 16:5-6; 19:1-7). This is an extension of the preceding point but given enough prominence as to be separately noticed. In recognizing the true worth of the God of reality they cannot help but sing his praise (W. Robert Cook, The Theology of John, pp. 246-48).

j)   Other instances: they were involved somehow, perhaps only as observers, in creation, (Job 38:4-7); they may be involved in the answer of prayer, (Dan. 9:20-23).

4.   Their names

a)   The Angel of Yahweh (see G. Vos, Biblical Theology. pp. 85- 89). This is probably a theophany or preincarnate appearance of Christ (doing the work of a messenger), i.e., it is the second person of the godhead who normally appears to men. See Genesis 16 and 18 for example. Thus, technically, this does not belong in a discussion of angelology.

b)   Gabriel ("the mighty one") (Luke 1:19, 26-38; Dan. 8:16; 9:21). He is always related to some special mission for God.

c)   Michael ("who is like God") (Rev. 12:7 and following; Dan, 10:21; 12:1; Jude 9). He is the only one called an archangel; the head of the armies of heaven; and is related to Israel in a special way.

d)   Cherubim (Gen. 3:24; Exod. 25:17-22; 26:31; Ezek. 28:14). They are first seen in Eden. Their likeness was on the mercy seat and in the veil. They seem to be defenders of God's holiness. It is possible that they should be identified with the four living creatures of Revelation 4:5 (cf. Ezek. 1:5-25; 10:20- 22).

e)   Seraphim (Isa. 6:2-7). They ascribe praise to God and are associated with the cleansing of a saint for service.

f)   Other. "Certain angels are known only by the service they render. Of these, there are those that sen·e as angels of judgment (Gen. 19:13; 2 Sam. 24:16; 2 Kings 19:35; Ezek. 9:1, 5, 7; Ps. 78:49). Account is made of the 'watcher' (Dan. 4:13, 23); 'angel of the abyss' (Rev. 9:11); 'angel over fire' (Rev. 14:18); 'angel of the waters' (Rev. 16:5); and of 'seven angels' (Rev. 8:2)" (L. S. Chafer, Systematic Theology. II, 20).

5. Their destiny

Revelation 5:11-14 and 21:12 suggest that they will continue into eternity.

B. Fallen Angels (other than Satan)

1. Their character

a)   They are evil and fallen (Job 4:18; Matt. 25:41; 2 Pet. 2:4; Jude 6; Rev. 9:11; 12:7-9). Since they are creatures, and all that God created was originally good, their evil character must have come subsequent to creation. If the "everything" of Genesis 1:31 be pressed to include the whole work of creation and not just the creation of the earth alone, then at this point on the sixth day everything, including angels, was good. Therefore, the fall of the angels must have been after creation week (See H. Bavinck, Our Reasonable Faith. p. 221).

b)   They know Christ (Matt. 8:29; Mark 1:23-24), but not savingly.

c)   They have an orthodox belief in God (James 2:19) which brings terror rather than life and peace.

d)   They are unclean and fierce (Matt. 10:1; 8:28).

2. Their activity

a)   Some are bound. A group of them are confined to Tartarus and kept for judgment (2 Pet. 2:4; Jude 6; cf. 1 Cor. 6:3; Rev. 20:10; Matt. 25:41). Since all are not bound it would appear that these are bound due to some specific sin.

Jude tells us that the reason they are being "kept in eternal bonds" is that they "did not keep their own domain, but abandoned their proper abode." This has been variously interpreted. Some have held that it refers to the sin of Genesis 6:1-4 (see discussion at the end of this chapter) while others have viewed it as describing a desire for more power and authority. Thiessen, commenting on the latter view states.

> It is assumed that God appointed one or more angels over each of the nations. The fact that various nations are thus under one or another of these angelic princes is clear from Daniel (10:13, 20 f.; 12:1). To leave their own principality (domain] might thus mean that they became unfaithful in the performance of their duties, but more probably it means that they sought to obtain a more coveted principality. To leave their proper habitation might mean that they left their heavenly dwelling and came down to earth (Lectures in Systematic Theology. revised, p. 140).

Erickson, on the other hand, rejects the idea that these verses teach that there are two classes of fallen angels.

> Another possibility is that these two verses describe the condition of all demons. . . . In verse 9 (of 2 Peter 2) Peter says that "the Lord knows how to rescue the godly from trial and to keep tbe unrighteous under punishment until the day of judgment." This language is almost identical to that used in verse 4. Note that the remainder of the chapter (vv. 10-22) is a description of the sinful activity of these people who are being kept under punishment. We conclude that, likewise, though cast into nether gloom, the fallen angels have sufficient freedom to carry on their evil activities (op. cit., p. 447).

If it is only the comparable statements between 2 Peter 2:4 and 9 that are noted, Erickson's view may be plausible. However, the sinning angels of verse 4 are "committed to Tartarus," a place of confinement, while the sinning humans of verses nine and following are not described as confined at all.

b)   Some are free (referred to as demons in the New Testament).

(1) Theories of origin. (a) They are disembodied spirits of evil men now deceased. Luke 16:22-31 and Revelation 20:13 disprove this theory for they show that evil human beings continue to be just that in eternity

and that they yet face a judgment of their own as humans not angels. (b) They are disembodied spirits of a pre-Adamic race. Scripture, however, teaches that Adam was the first man (Gen. 2:7; 1 Cor. 15:45) and that all things were created within creation week (Exod. 20:11). (c) They are disembodied spirits of the "nephilim" of Genesis 6. This concept is set forth in the apocryphal book of 1 Enoch, chapter 15. This describes the illicit union of angels (sons of God) and women. From this union it is held that both forbidden knowledge (magic) and demonic spirits issued. This idea is extra-biblical and contradicts biblical evidence which links the fall of angels (demons) with the fall of Satan. (d) Fallen angels are demons. A comparison of Matthew 12:24-27, where Satan is seen as prince of demons, with Matthew 25:41, which speaks of the devil and his angels, seems to identify the two. While it is true that the two are never expressly identified, neither are they clearly distinguished. The two do share certain common characteristics such as the ability to possess the bodies of depraved men (cf. John 13:27 and Luke 11:23-26; see also Rev. 9:11 and con text).

(2) Their work. (Note well they are Satan's angels, Matt. 25:41; Rev. 12:7-9, and he is their prince, Matt. 12:22-26, thus their work is his work.) (a) They seem to be bodiless spirits which need, or at least greatly desire, to be embodied to exercise maximum control (Mark 5:1-13; Luke 11:24-26). (b) They are many in number and thus make Satan appear to be omnipotent, omniscient, and omnipresent (Luke 8:30) as they work with him in carrying out his plans (Eph. 6:11-12; Rev. 12:7-12). (c) They can cause physical and mental disease or aberrations, such as dumbness, blindness, insanity, great physical strength (Matt. 9:32-33; 12:22; Mark 5:4-5; Luke 8:35; 9:37-42; cf. 2 Cor. 12:7). Having noted these facts, and without minimizing them, two cautions are needed. In the first place, all illness should not be attributed to demonic activity. *A5* Erickson observes,

> It is noteworthy that the biblical writers did not attribute all illness to demon possession. Luke reports that Jesus distinguished between two types of healing: "Behold, I cast out demons and perform cures today and tomorrow" (Luke 13:32). A similar distinction is made in Matthew 10:8; Mark 1:34; 6:13; Luke 4:40-41; 9:1. Nor was epilepsy mistaken for demon possession. We read in Matthew 17:15-18 that Jesus cast out a demon from an epileptic, but in Matthew 4:24 epileptics (as well as paralytics) are distinguished from demoniacs (op. cit., pp. 449-50).

Secondly, and actually a corollary of the first caution, we should be very careful today about concluding that mental illness is the result of demon activity. There are doubtless examples in contemporary society of demonically induced mental imbalance but many times the causes are physical or emotional. (d) They may inflict personal injury (Luke 9:38, 39, 42). (e) They may lead into immorality. Probably all references to "unclean" spirits suggest this idea in light of the fact that the term akathartos often is used this way and that being spirits without physical bodies it must refer to moral impurity (cf. 1 Tim. 4:1-3). (f) They disseminate false doctrine (2 Thess. 2:2; 1 Tim. 4:1; 1 John 4:1-3; cf. 2 Cor. 11:14-15). (g) They oppose the life and ministry of believers (Rom. 8:38-39; Eph. 6:12). (h) They have power to work "miracles" (Rev. 13:12-15; 16:14; cf. 2 Thess. 2:9 where the statement is not about bogus miracles but miracles, signs and wonders in support of falsehood as in Matt. 24:24). (i) They encourage idolatry (1 Cor. 10:20; Rev. 9:20; cf. 2 Thess. 2:3, 4, 9). (j) They influence human governments (Dan. 10:13-20; Eph. 6:12). **(k)** They work in opposition to unfallen angels (Dan. 10:12-13). (1) There apparently was increased demon activity during the life of our Lord on earth and will be again in the end times prior to his second coming (Rev. 9:20; 13:4; 16:13-14; 2 Thess. 2:9). (m) God sometimes uses them to accomplish his purposes (Judges 9:23; 1 Kings 22:20-23; Ps. 78:49).

(3) Their manifestation.

Demons serve Satan in a variety of ways. These demonstrate his consuming desire to thwart God's purposes and establish his own kingdom. Thiessen identifies three categories of demonology. The first may be broadly categorized as fortune-telling. This includes such things as ouija boards, tarot cards, tea leaves, palm reading and gazing in a crystal ball.

> On the lowest plane, this may be mere human foresight, studied deception, or pure superstition. In biblical times there was augury or foretelling of the future by means of natural signs, such as the flight of birds or the disposition of the entrails (Ezek. 21:21), hydromancy or foretelling from the appearance of the water poured into a vessel or of objects dropped into the water (Gen. 44:5), and astrology or the determination of the supposed influence of the stars on the destiny of a person (Isa. 47:13) (op. cit., p. 146).

Since these are all attempts to know the future apart from divine disclosure they are at the least demonic in character and when such information is actually forthcoming they are demonic in fact (see Acts 16:16).

The second category involves actual demon worship. Various pagan religious rites, voodoo and modern satan cults fall into this grouping. "Apostate Israel sacrificed to demons (Deut. 32:17; Ps.

106:37). Food sacrificed to idols in New Testament times was actually sacrificed to demons (1 Cor. 10:19 f.)" (ibid.).

The third category is sometimes referred to as spiritualism but is better designated spiritism. "Spiritism is the belief that the living can communicate with the dead and that the spirits of the dead can manifest their presence to men. Necromancy, as this is called, is supposedly done through the agency of a human being known as a medium" (ibid.). Witches, warlocks and magicians (not those involved in prestidigitation) are manifestations of this kind of demonism (see e.g., 1 Sam. 28:3-14; Acts 8:9-24; 13:6-9). Israel was commanded by God not to consult with such as these at peril of death (Lev. 19:31; 20:6, 27; Dt. 18:10-12; 2 Kings 21:6; 1 Chron. 10:13; Isa. 8:19).

This service of Satan may evidence itself at two levels and the various demonic works may be carried on at either one.

(a) Demon possession. One of the most terrifying and perplexing evidences of demonic activity is demon possession. It involves demonic control of the individual from within and may be viewed as the unholy counterpart of the filling of the Holy Spirit. From the standpoint of God's original intention for human beings it may be viewed as a transgression and violation of the person, that is of the <u>imago dei.</u> "That (demons] possess individuals is part of their continuing effort to frustrate the program of God, rather than merely a desire to be clothed with a human body" (op. cit., p. 141). Demon possession may bring a variety of effects and be evidenced in widely divergent ways. It may evidence itself in mental derangement or superhuman physical strength and may lead to bodily harm (Mark 5:1-5). One who is demon possessed may function as a medium (Acts 16:16-18) or a clergyman (2 Cor. 11:12-15). On occasion there are multiple possessions (Mark 5:9; Luke 8:2) and there are degrees of control (Matt. 12:45). Often there is close psychological identification between the victim and the demon (Mark 1:23-26; 5:6-12).

Probably the most vexing question relating to this subject is, who can be possessed? It has been suggested that "the fact that they 'seek' rest (see Matt. 12:43; Luke 11:24] would indicate that they cannot possess just anyone. They apparently cannot violate the will of an intended victim and so seek those who willingly yield themselves to their evil influences" (C. R. Smith, "The New Testament Doctrine of Demons," <u>Grace Journal.</u> Spring 1969). It would appear, however, from Mark 9:21, that there may be exceptions to this. The term translated "from a child" literally means from the time of early childhood and allows for the possibility that it was at a time before such willful choice of evil would be exercised. While Smith's analysis may be generally true, we need to recognize, as Merrill Unger suggests, that "there may be special divine permission of unusual Satanic operation to accomplish some extraordinary purpose of divine wisdom in accordance with the principles of the divine sovereignty" (Biblical Demonology. p. 95).

There is no question that unbelievers may be and sometimes are possessed by demons. There is ample biblical evidence as well as experiential data to support this. But what about the believer? Experience seems to suggest that they may, but is there any biblical evidence of such a possibility and is it theologically compatible with Christian doctrine? It is argued by many, without any specific biblical teaching as support, that believers cannot be demonized or possessed because they are indwelt by the Holy Spirit; and, two spirits, one evil and the other holy, cannot indwell the same person at the same time. Thus, to be indwelt by the Holy Spirit is held to be guarantee against demon possession. This assertion, however, is just that and remains to be demonstrated. Also, since demon control is not necessarily permanent it is questionable that it should be paralleled to the indwelling of the Spirit which is permanent. Others have claimed that there are no biblical examples of a believer being possessed by a demon although, as will be noted below, Ananias (Acts 5:3) may well be such a person. It is true that there are no examples of sinful believers being exorcised and there is no command to exorcise such but this is strictly an argument from silence. Also it loses any force that it may have in light of the fact that there is no command to exorcise anybody in the scriptures.

A more compelling argument in support of this view is found by reference to such passages as John 17:15 where Christ prays that the Father will keep his own from the evil one; Romans 8:38-39 where Paul declares that angels cannot separate us from the love of God in Christ Jesus our Lord; and Colossians 1:13 where Paul declares that we have been rescued from the authority of darkness.

There does seem to be some evidence, on the other hand, in at least one case, of a believer being demon controlled. The term daimonidzomai, to be under the power of a demon (e.g., Matt. 15:22), is not used of one who is clearly identified as a believer although in most cases of its use there is nothing in the context, apart from the demon possession itself, to suggest that they are not. In Acts 5:3 Peter says of Ananias that Satan, a demon or fallen angel, "filled his heart." This verb is clearly used metaphorically much as it is in Ephesians 5:18 of the Holy Spirit. In both places it means "control." It may be questioned as to whether Ananias was a believer but the context clearly establishes that he was a member of the church in Jerusalem. Also, the death of Ananias and Sapphira brought "great fear" upon the church as well as upon others and if it were unbelievers being judged it is questionable that the church would have been thus affected.

It would appear, then, that disobedience to divine revelation (as with Ananias and Sapphira who lied to God the Holy Spirit and agreed together to test the Holy Spirit, Acts 5:3-4, 9) <u>may</u> open one to such control. But, at the same time, it is of utmost importance to remember that the way in for the demon is the way out of demon control for the believer. Just as willful disobedience may bring it on so willing obedience to God's word will bring deliverance and protection. The passages referred to above as possibly precluding demon possession (John 17:15; Rom. 8:38- 39; Col. 1:13; together v.ith 1 John 4:4) do not necessarily guarantee that demons may not temporarily control the believer but they do guarantee that any control they do exercise is limited and temporary.

Whether one believes that believers may be demon possessed or not there are, nonetheless, people who are so controlled. What is the biblical pattern for exorcism or is there one? There are several instances in the New Testament of the exorcism of demons although there is no direct instruction as to how exorcism is to be conducted. On some occasions the demon being exorcised leaves the victim with reluctance (Matt. 12:27; Mark 9:26). There are examples of Jesus removing demons with a command (Mark 1:25; 9:25) and on other occasions he says that he casts them out by the Spirit of God (Matt. 12:28), that is the finger of God (Luke 11:20). His authority to cast out demons was inherent and was often acknowledged by the demons themselves. The disciples, on the other hand, had a derived authority, given by the Lord (Matt. 10:1, 8). In some instances their ability to function this way was hindered by their lack of faith (Matt. 17:19-20) and in others our Lord's activity was curtailed by lack of faith in others (Mark 9:23-24; cf. 6:5-6). On another occasion prayer was said to be vital (Mark 9:29). It is evident from this data that there is no set formula or pattern in the scripture for exorcism but that the authority of Jesus Christ, trust in God and prayer are characteristic aspects of this exercise.

Because of the inordinate fascination that some evidence for exorcism a word of caution is in order. It is a serious aspect of one's ministry. Nowhere is the Christian commissioned to cast out demons. Unless one accepts the validity of the long ending of Mark's gospel (16:17) there is nothing more than a descriptive record of exorcisms that have taken place in the scripture. This does leave open the possibility of such activity but does not give it prominence. Even our Lord's ministry did not place the focus here and on one occasion, when it became apparent to him that his disciples were being unduly attracted toward exorcism he cautioned them ·with a mild rebuke. Luke records, "And the seventy returned with joy, saying, 'Lord, even the demons are subject to us in your name.' And he said ... 'do not rejoice in this, that the spirits are subject to you, but rejoice that your names are recorded in heaven'" (Luke 10:17-20). In other words, without denying the validity of such a ministry whereby Satan is defeated, he reminded them that something else is of far greater importance. Our commission is to make disciples not to cast out demons.

(b) Demon influence. In contrast to demon possession, demon influence refers to external demonic activity from outside an individual through pressure, suggestion, and temptation. Such activity is with a view to the hindrance of God's purposes for mankind and the extension of Satan's sphere of authority. Among other things this involves the misleading of the unbelievers (2 Cor. 11:13-15) and the waging of war upon the believer (Eph. 6:12).

(c) The believer's defense against the activity of demons. The Bible gives very strong prohibition of every form of the occult. The reason is that it is so closely related to demonic activity. In Deuteronomy 18:9-22. God not only pronounces these pagan practices as detestable he also says that any of his people who practice them are detestable to him. The point of the passage seems to be that God's people are not to rely upon any other source for guidance or any other word of authority than that from God himself. For this reason, he says he will raise up his spokesman who will speak his message as his prophet. Today the completed scriptures serve that function •for us for with the coming of Christ, the prophet greater than Moses, the last word has been spoken.

This strong prohibition regarding occult knowledge includes astrology, as well. As Isaiah records God's proscription of Babylon's errors he includes astrology along with sorceries and magic spells (Isa. 47:13-15). From the beginning stars are presented in scripture as created by God and thus subject to him. They were appointed to govern day and night not to govern men's lives (Gen. 1:16-17) That is God's province alone·.

3. <u>Their destiny</u>

a)   Temporary. The intermediate destiny of the bound fallen angels is Tartarus (Greek text) (2 Pet. 2:4); or the abyss (Luke 8:31; Rev. 9:1-11; 20:1-3).

b)   Final. The ultimate destiny of all fallen angels is the lake of fire (Matt. 25:41).

4. The problem of Genesis 6:1-4

Another puzzling problem relating to the doctrine of fallen angels relates to Genesis 6:1-4. Does the reference to "sons of God" have angels or human beings in view? Unlike the problems surrounding demon possession one's view on this issue has little theological or practical ramifications.

a)   The "Sethite" hypothesis.

1. This was first seriously proposed by Augustine although probably held earlier by Chrysostom. It was held by Calvin, Hengstenberg, Keil, Matthew Henry, Scofield, and G. Vos.

2. It seems to have the strength of the preceding context in that there is no mention of angels up to this point in Genesis (see, however, 3:24). Also, Seth's line seems to be presented as the godly line--chapter 4 shows the Cainites and Sethites divided; chapter 5 presents the Sethites in devotedness; chapter 6 sets forth the mingling of the two lines. Genesis 4:26 pictures the godliness of the Sethites.

3. The term "sons of God" refers to unfallen angels or to believers in the Old Testament and this in the later literature (Isa. 43:6; Job 1:6; 2:1). In the historical literature angels are never styled by this term.

4. Intermarriage between angels and men is impossible, (Matt. 22:30).

5. The results of the wedlock were nothing unusual (as claimed by some who hold the other view). The text says Nephilim "were" not "came to be" on the earth. Also, there were Nephilim later on (Num. 13:33) so how can it be said that they were destroyed in the flood?

6. According to verse 3 the judgment is upon men only. Jude 6 and 2 Peter 2:4 refer to a prehistoric incident. The Jude 6 passage teaches that Israel sinned through unbelief in the divine revelation, angels sinned against the divine ordinance which gave them a certain position as they sought after greater dominion, and that the Sodomites sinned against the divine laws of sexual relationship. The three judgments of these three instances are distinct from one another. The statement "in like manner with these" is to be related to "set forth as an example" while the words "given themselves over to fornication and gone after strange flesh" are parenthetical and refer only to the Sodomites. This view holds that the sin which brought the flood was the breaking down of the line of demarcation between the godly and the ungodly.

b)   The "angel" hypothesis.

1. Every time the title "sons of God" is used in the Old Testament it refers to angels. The type of literature in which it occurs is of no particular significance. The passages used to prove that believers are so named in the Old Testament do not use this title. Believers are nowhere in the Old Testament called sons of God in this phraseology (bne elohim or bne hael).

2. There is no evidence that the term "daughters of men" should be limited to Cainites.

3. This view alone accounts for the sudden appearance of and enigmatic reference to the Nephilim (fallen ones). Otherwise there is no reason to mention them. (There is no reason from this context to think that they were giants. This is inferred from Numbers 13:32-33. Also, the LXX does read gigantes here.) These may be a reference to the unusual progeny of this union or to "fallen ones," that is, depraved men who subjected themselves to demon possession and in turn cohabited with the daughters of men. The progeny then would be those referred to in verse 4 as mighty men of renown (cf. Gen. 10:8-9; Mark 5:2-4). The occurrence of Nephilim in Numbers 13 does not mean that they survived the flood, nor even that they are of the same type of union, but merely that there were those who could be thus described (cf. the use of the term hagioi in the New Testament both of saints and angels).

4. Matthew 22:30 is not intended to prove anything other than the fact that with resurrection bodies men will not procreate human babies just as angels do not produce angelic offspring. It does not rule out the possibility of angels with assumed bodies cohabiting with women and producing some sort of abnormal human progeny.

5. Some versions of the LXX use angeloi here, indicating that the translators held this view.

6. Jude 6-7 suggest that the sin of Sodom and Gomorrah was like (hōs) that of angels. Toutois, "with these," refers back to angels in verse 6 grammatically, not to the word cities (see Alford, Lenski, Robertson, in loc.). The flesh for which the Sodomites lusted was "strange (heteras) flesh" and Genesis 19 indicates that this did include angels. No specific biblical explanation of the angels leaving their proper habitation is given by any other view.

7. 2 Peter 2:4-5 refers to Tartarus as a special place of confinement for the angels who did the things there attributed to them and this view accounts for the need for such a place.

8. History gives an answer to the change from the angel view to the other. (a) One of the Ante-Nicene fathers, Julius Africanus, proposed the other view but it was not accepted until Augustine. (b) It was accepted from Augustine's time, as he set it forth, because of the philosophic setting of the day. Greek mythology said that there was an unholy union between the gods of heaven and the goddesses of earth which brought forth monstrosities that were in turn cast into Tartarus. (c) Since the two stories resembled each other, Augustine

and others were embarrassed and tried to explain the incident otherwise. (9) This view has been held by Justin, Tertullian, Cyprian, Lactantius; Delitzsch, Stier, Kelly, Luther, Pember, Gaebelein. Unger, Ryrie. See U. Cassuto, <u>Biblical and Oriental Studies,</u> I, 17-28 for an extended statement of this view.

This view holds that Satan was in this way attempting to pollute the line through which Christ was to come (cf. Gen. 3:15), and that God sent the flood because of the extreme wickedness in the earth and to destroy the resultant creatures of this cohabitation.

c)   The "nobleman" hypothesis. Without elaborating it, brief reference should be made to a third viewpoint recently advanced by Meredith Kline. This is a restatement of an ancient Jewish interpretation which holds that the "sons of god" refers to Cainite kings or nobles. In this view the "daughters of men" are women in general and the sin for which the earth was judged is rampant polygamy. In Kline's article ("Divine Kingship and Genesis 6:1-4," <u>(Westminster Theological Journal,</u> May, 1962, pp. 187-204) his primary concern is to state this alternative view. Leroy Birney ("An Exegetical Study of Genesis 6:1-4," <u>Journal of the Evangelical Theological Society,</u> Winter, 1970, 43-52) also supports this view. He gives a very summary)· and inadequate treatment of the "angel" hypothesis and dismisses it much too easily. His treatment of the "Sethite" view is much more sympathetic.

ABOUT THE AUTHOR

Lowry Edwards Foster was born in Great Bend, Kansas, and grew up in Garden City immersed in music and sports. After college at the University of Arkansas and a brief football career, he went to graduate school in Portland, Oregon.

Returning to Arkansas, he settled in Little Rock, where his love for running grew. Lowry Edwards, who now lives in Evergreen, Colorado, continues to inspire others through his writing, art, and lifelong passion for fitness.